Miracles

Flairs and Glairs
Publication House

"Miracles"

ISBN No: " 978-93-90416-00-4"
1st Edition
Language – English and Hindi

Flairs and Glairs
Publication House
Regd. Under MSME Act.

Disclaimer

This is a work of fiction and solely represent the thoughts of the corresponding authors of the articles. Our editors have tried their best to edit the content of all the authors and check the plagiarism.
All the write-ups in this book are unique and are only published in this book.
In case any plagiarism or error is found, only the author is responsible alone, and not the publisher or the Compilers.

Cover Designing and Book Formatting
Shubham Shah and Ishani Agarwal

Acknowledgement

Dear Almighty, thank you for blessing me with the power and zeal to be able to complete this Anthology. Also, Thank You dear parents and my loved ones for trusting in me, and letting me work whenever I wanted. My family is the one who supported me for what I am today. When it comes to this Anthology, I would like to start with thanking the Co-authors, without your help and support, I would have never been able to complete it. Thank You all of you, for being there. Much Love to all of you. I am glad to see you all standing by me.

Co-authors

Shubham Shah (Founder, Flairs and Glairs)
Ishani Agarwal (Co-Founder, Flairs and Glairs)
Shruthi Basam (Compiler)

1. Abhilash Rout
2. Abhiraj Gautam
3. Ajay Chaursiya
4. Amit Kumar Ray
5. Ananya Patra
6. Ankit Shekhar
7. Ankita Hundekar
8. Apurva Srivastava
9. Anisha Mishra
10. Asha Manish Singh
11. Akhila Bongi
12. Archita Mahajan
13. Anchal Srivastava
14. Ashuthosh Singh
15. Ankeeta Sahani
16. Ashwini Prasad
17. Baisakhi Das
18. Chetan Bansor
19. Dr Rakesh R Mund
20. Debanjana Ghatak
21. Divya Rajiv Jain
22. Disita Sikidar
23. Dipti David
24. Deepti Srivastava
25. Dheeraj Davarya
26. Dhanush
27. Dr Gunjan Arya

28. Dr Rucha Mavadiya
29. Eshika Kumari
30. E Pavithra
31. Gorang Choubisa
32. Gousia Ajaz Khan
33. Gopal Chanchlani
34. G.B Nandhini
35. Gayathri.S
36. Gyanendra Rajeev Singh
37. Gunjan Jogia
38. Hasrat Garg
39. Harshil Soni
40. Ishrat Jahan Noormohammed Khan
41. Imran Shaikh
42. Jeevitha.S
43. Jyoti Kukreja
44. Jata V
45. Kiran Khasiya
46. Kavitha P
47. Kiran Kumari
48. Kumari Tripti
49. Kavita Malviya
50. Keerthi Sai Sharanya Suggala
51. Keerthana Suriya
52. K Sudheendra Nayak
53. Lahari Shetty
54. Monisha Ray
55. Muskan Godara
56. Meenakshi Periyasamy
57. Mamta
58. M. Meharun Halidha
59. Namisha Barik
60. Navneet
61. Neeraj
62. Om Prakash Lovevanshi 'Sangam'
63. Pramesh Kumar

64. Priyanka Rupreja
65. Prittam Bhattacharyya
66. Payal Surani
67. Pragathishri Shanthi
68. Riddhi Lodha
69. Ritika Sharma
70. Rashmi Maurya
71. Rupakshi Dadhich
72. Rohit Lakhavatri
73. Rohit Kumar
74. Roneeca Brajasundar Sahu
75. Swati Pahad
76. Samparnna Dalbehera
77. Shijin Ravi
78. Subhransu Padhy
79. Swati Kumari
80. Saptak Baral
81. Shaikh S Shohel
82. Sybil Samuel
83. Sukrurtha B
84. Sanjay Naik
85. Shobika Balaraman
86. Sandhya A.S.
87. Saima Anwer
88. Sana Maheboob
89. Sakshi Jain
90. Sachin Banoudhiya
91. Shreyas Sahay
92. Shalini G S
93. Shubham
94. Shivansh Mishra
95. Swapnali Jagtap
96. S.K.Vishnu Prasath
97. Saarthak
98. Tejaswini Kuppalla
99. Upasana Borbora

100. Nasreena Khan
101. Vashisth Dave

Shubham Shah

(Founder- Flairs and Glairs)

Shubham Shah, an entrepreneur at “Flairs & Glairs” a brand with dynamics in events organizing and cultural educational pan INDIA, is a 26yrs old guy who recently has entered the digital platform of imprinting emotions. He has initiated with his own open mic platform to help budding poets and aspiring writers under his brand named as “Teekhe Zasbaaat”

He is a commerce graduate from the Bhagalpur City of Bihar. He states Writing has impersonated him since childhood and he has now been writing for over a decade!
Cooking, on the other hand, is his passion! He also mentions, trying out new things just tickles him!
When asked sir, Why SPICY EMOTIONS?
He smiled and added, "agar jasbaat teekhe na ho toh wo jasbaat kahan" Spices are all that blends! So do his words!
As a chef, he presents to you his dish! Hot and freshly served! Taste it! Feel it! Enjoy it! You can also find his writing in the Book "Teekhe Zasbaaat" and 50+ Co-authored anthologies. With his passion to explore opportunities across Platforms, he is working with keen devotion and We wish him all the very best for his future ventures.
He is Featured in the **International Magazine De-Mode** for his upcoming solo novel.
He is **Approved by Ne8x for its Lit Fest,** and is a **Golden Star Awards 2020 Winner.**
He is an **India Book of Records Holder** for his Anthology **Satrang,** and has the **Grandmaster** title by **Asia Book of Records**, for the same.
He has also been featured in **Prabhat Khabar**, **Dainik Jagran** and other renowned Newspaper for his achievements. He has also been awarded with **India Star Republic Award 2021.**
He has been a proud co-author to
India Book of Records (Title- Black)
World Book of Records (Title -15 Wonders of Poetries)
India Book of Records (Title - Aaina)
Vajra World Records Holder (Title - Gustakhi Maaf Hai)
High Range of Records Holder (Title - Gustakhi Maaf Hai)

Share your reviews on his

INSTAGRAM

@spicy_emotions
@shubham4shah

Or via email on

shubham2shah@gmail.com

To stay tuned to his work and opportunities follow his business Handles

INSTAGRAM FACEBOOK YOUTUBE

@flairsandglairs
@teekhezasbaaat

WEBSITE:

https://flairsandglairs.in/
https://flairsandglairs.com/

Ishani Agarwal

(Co-Founder- Flairs and Glairs)

Ishani Agarwal hails from the City of Joy, Kolkata.
She is the co-founder of her Community "Teekhe Zasbaaat" and Flairs and Glairs Publication.
Been a Compiler for 45+ Anthologies, she is in the process for more. Co-authored in 150+ Anthologies. She is a India Book of Records Holder, a Vajra World Records Holder, a High Range of Records Holder and a Bravo Record holder.

Approved by Ne8x for its Lit Fest 2020, and Literary Icon 2020. Also a Golden Star Awards Winner 2020.

She has also been awarded with India Star Republic Award 2021.

She has been featured by the National Magazine "Taree Zameen Par" with the title 'unstoppable'.

Also featured in the International Magazine DeMode for her upcoming solo novel, she is proud to write on social issues, and is happy with the love she is receiving.

Connect with her on Instagram: @Ishani_agarwal_quotes / @compilations_so_far

Shruthi Basam

(Compiler)

Shruthi Basam hails from Mumbai, Maharashtra. She is currently pursuing Bachelors in Pharmacy. She also opens herself as an anthology compiler. She has co-authored several anthologies titled “Silent Sunset”, “Shh”, “Poetic Shadow”, “Artsy of Words” etc. Also, she has been a part of World Record Anthology named “BLACK” in which she received India Book of Records. She writes poems and quotes to heal her heart and make her sorrows disappear. Her 1st compilation book is already launched 'SILENT TEARS'.

You

Even though you are far from me
My heart feels you near.
I feel comfort in your arms
You take away all my fears.
Your eyes sparkle like a star in sky
When I stare into them .
I feel like I'm soaring high
I never stop thinking of you.
You brought me sunshine
When I only saw rain
You brought me laughter
When I only felt pain.
I believe in fate and destiny
But I also believe
We are only fated
To do things together.

Miracles

We, as human beings expect some super
natural power to work for us,
but we always forget that our breath is itself
a miracle from God.
The reason behind this is that many person,
want to enjoy this beautiful day but due to
some reasons they could not enjoy as
they are stuck in their beds and struggling
with the last stage of some dangerous
diseases or maybe for some other reasons.
We should always remain greatful to God.
For this wonderful life and we should always
expect according to our needs and not
according to our comforts because God
has the power to do miracles in our life
when we submit ourselves in his feets.
God is able to change from nothing to everything,
but he will start doing from the
very next moment when we start
surrendering ourselves and start living a
lifestyle according to his wills and not
according to our comforts.

ख्वाबों का जहां

वहां लगे कुछ अपना सा,
जो था एक सपना था,
उसे पूरा कर जाना है,
इसे सच बनाना है,
एक जहां बसाना है,
उसे अपनों से सजाना है,
वहां मोहब्बत बरसाना है,
सारे रिश्तो को निभाना है,
वहां एक छोटा बगीचा हो,
हमने जिसे प्यार से सिचा हो,
वहां एक छोटा सा माकान हो,
खाने को दो वक़्त का पकवान हो,
जहां सब दुःख-दर्द से अनजान हो,
जहां सिर्फ खुशियों का निर्माण हो।

Ajay Chaursiya

Unsaid

Her love for him like a rain for land
When raining more there's no sign of sand
When it stands UNSAID it leaves only dirt
And after disappearance they make desert
In between these it shows some stain of love
Which gives them peace after storm as dove
Black left their places and make it for sun
Finally, it all ends killing one with winter gun

Yaadein

Tere sath bitayi har yaad likh liya
Tune kahi thi jo
Wo har baat likh liya....
Jo karta hu tujhse
Wo ishq beshumar karna hai
Han tujhse hi ab pyaar karna hai.....

Aur me likhta nhi hu ab
Tujhe likhte likhte
Alfaaz bhi kam pad gaye....
Ab to bas ishq ka intezar karna hai
Han tujhse hi ab pyaar karna hai….

Dear Me

A small letter for you,
Let go of the idea of perfection. Accept the fact that you can't be perfect, you just can be real. Let yourself to be flawed, allow yourself to do mistakes. Accept the fact that you are not going to have it all together. Sometimes your heart is going to break and you are going to get hurt. You are going to feel pain but don't apologize for being broken. Every time you break you become a little more alive. You become more open to yourself, you become exposed to your sensibility. Every scar will tell you a little more about your struggle, your strength, your courage. Don't hide it from the world. They are also a part of it. The most beautiful people are beautifully broken. Their hearts are heavy but they love the deepest. It's a beautiful ***Miracle*** to be alive in this world. Our chance of being here are nearly zero but we are here. So, live the life you want to live.

Ankit Shekhar

जिसके आने का गम ना हो
उसके लिए तराशना बेकार है।।

बून्द-बून्द पानी का मोल ना हो
उस घड़ा का बनना बेकार है।

धागों की बुनाई को परखा ना हो
उस कमीज़ का बिखना बेकार है।

स्याही की लेखनी का महत्व ना हो
उस पन्नो को पढ़ना बेकार है।

अग्नि की जलन में तृप्ता ना हो
उस रोशनी का फैलना बेकार है।

ज्ञान की प्राणी में समझ ना हो
उस गुण को आचरण में लाना बेकार है।

जिसके आने का गम ना हो
उसके लिए तराशना बेकार है।।

Welcome to The Land of Pretending!!

Good people around with faking talks! Depression, problems and conflicts everywhere. Money and materialism ruling over. Every night with moist eye, every rise with a huge fake smile, pretending to be all good! Dark everywhere, fake people engulfing all the light! Chained with circumstances. Buried with unwanted emotions!

Apurva Srivastava

फुर्सत की शाम

फुर्सत की एक शाम हो,
कुछ फरेबी और कुछ बेईमान हो,
कुछ शरारतें भी मंजूर हो,
कुछ गलतियां भी माफ हो,
कुछ याद रहे कुछ भूल जाएं
इस कदर तुझ में घुल जाए।
कुछ दूर कदम मिलाकर देखें,
तेरे कांधे पर सर सजा कर देखें।
कुछ कहो जो हम दिल से लगा कर बैठें।
कोई वक्त का ना हिसाब ले,
ये शाम ढल भी जाए ना कोई ऐलान हो।
बस इतना सा सुकून तेरे साथ हो,
फुर्सत की एक शाम हो...

Anisha Mishra

There is always a pinch of doubt,
in the world of goodness.
But,
there is always a hope of care,
in the world of dark.

लाडली सास

एक परिवार में तीन बेटे थे और उनके मां-बाप। उनमें से दो बेटों की शादी हो गई थी, दोनों बहुएं अपनी सास को बहुत प्यार करती थी। सास घर की लाडली थी, उसे जरा भी तकलीफ होती तो पूरा घर सर पर उठा लेती थी और सारा दिन घर में बैठे अपनी सेवा करवाती थी दोनों बहुओं से ,और घर का कोई काम नहीं करती थी। और दोनों बहुएं भी सारा दिन घर का काम करती और अपनी सास की सेवा करती अपने सास के नखरे भी उठाती थी। तभी कुछ दिनों बाद तीसरे बेटी की भी शादी हो जाति है , तीसरी बहू जब घर में आई ब्याह के तो उसने क्या देखा कि सास को सब लोग बहुत प्यार करते हैं, और सास को जरा भी तकलीफ नहीं होने देते थे और नाराज भी नहीं होने देते थे हमेशा खुश रखते थे और सास को खुश रखने के लिए परेशान भी रहते थे, उसे थोड़ी हैरानी हुई ये सब देख कर उसने ठान लिया ,की इसका पता जरूर लगाएगी, एक दिन सास ने छोटी बहू को काम दिया तो बहू ने इंकार कर दिया वह कहने लगी मैं क्यों करूं आप करो आप तो दिन भर बैठी रहती हो और फिर तब क्या था सास जोर जोर से चिल्लाने लगी पूरा घर सर पर उठा लिया तभी पूरा परिवार भागता हुआ आया और पूछने लगा क्या हुआ क्यों परेशान हो रही हो तुम शांत रहो गुस्सा मत करो दिमाग शांत करो। यह सब देख बहू को कुछ अजीब लगा फिर सब के जाने के बाद सास ने छोटी बहू से कहा देखा! मैं अगर परेशान होती हूं तो पूरा घर मेरे पीछे परेशान हो जाता है। तभी, बहू ने सोचा मैं इसका पर्दाफाश करके रहूंगी। और एक दिन उसने अपनी सास को फोन पर किसी से बात करते हुए सुना, उसने सुना कि उसकी सास किसी से कह रही थी पंडित जी मैं आपको लाखों रुपए देती हूं ताकि आप सबको यह बताओ कि अपनी सास को खुश रखना है नहीं तो लक्ष्मी चली जाएंगी इस घर से रूठ

कर और जो भी इस घर में पैसे आते हैं वह मेरी खुश रहने की वजह से ही आते हैं। और अचानक सबका प्यार कैसे कम होने लगा ,इतना पैसा देने के बावजूद आप मेरा काम क्यों नहीं कर रहे हो, आपने तो कहा था यह पूजा करवाने के बाद सब लोग मुझसे बहुत प्यार करेंगे। तभी छोटी बहू यह सारी बातें सुन लेती है ,और सोच लेती है कि मैं सभी घरवालों को यह बात बताऊंगी और अपनी सास का पर्दाफाश कर के रहूंगी फिर क्या था, छोटी बहू एक प्लान बनाती है। चुपके से उस पंडित को घर पर बुलाती है और बाकी घर वालों को छुपने के लिए केह देती है तभी पंडित आता है और उससे कहता है मैंने तो काम कर दिया था। उसकी सांस बोलती ह,मै हर महीने आपको लाखों रुपए भेजती हूं पहले साइकिलि थी आपके पास अभी कार हो गई है तभी, सभी घरवाले चुपके से उसकी सारी बातें सुन लेते हैं बहू के ससुर बहुत नाराज होते हैं कि तुम मुझसे हर महीने पैसे लेती थी इस धोखेबाज को देने के लिए! फिर क्या था छोटी बहू के ससुर बहुत नाराज होते हैं उसकी सास पर और तीनों बेटे भी नाराज हो जाते अपनी मां से और कहने लगते हैं आज के बाद तुम घर के कामों में हाथ बटाओगी और और अपनी बहू की मदद भी करोगी, इस घर में जो भी पैसे आ रहे हैं वह तुम्हारे खुश रहने से नहीं हमारे मेहनत करने से आए हैं। और इस तरीके से वह अपनी सास का पर्दाफाश करती है। फिर सास को भी समझ आजाता है कि प्यार हासिल करने के लिए किसी पूजा पाठ करने की जरूरत नहीं है बल्कि हमें सब के साथ मिल-जुल कर रहना चाहिए, प्रेम-व्यवहार के साथ रहना चाहिए। उसके बाद वह तीनों बहू के साथ खुशी-खुशी काम में हाथ बटाती है ,और साथ में सभी खुशी-खुशी रहने लगते हैं।

शिक्षा- "अगर हमें सम्मान और प्यार चाहिए तो बदले में हमें भी दूसरों को उतना ही प्यार और सम्मान देना चाहिए"।।

Your Thoughts - Your Weapons

We are born a miracle,
Miracles arise from our thoughts,
When we are honest in our work and humble in the way we behave,
we look great,
Miracles take a long time to happen,
Everyday routines such as breathing, walking, working, etc. are
miraculous,
But we do not even think of them that way, because they have become commonplace in our lives,
But when some people are out of breath ... their life will stand still if they breathe all at once,
Some things do not even reach our imagination but stand as evidence for the continuation of our life in that matter.. Our efficiency in using the opportunity that comes is evident, Our skill is in making the expected opportunities come, Only believe in yourself in this world .. The one moment you take for granted how your life will be is what drives the rest of your life,
There is nothing wrong with taking the advice of others when making any decision,
But counsellors recognize that they are not the cause of any of the decisions you make...

Archita Mahajan

Metaphorical Quotes

1. Even the sun doesn't fail to provide light to the moon, and you expect the right person to leave you in the darkness?

2. Rose may give you petals and thorns, but I, I'll only give you peace and no storms.

3. Real beauty is not the shine the moon steals from the sun, but the darkness it has from within.

4. A relationship can only be constant, when the effort is two sided; Even a shooting star needs gravity to be guided.

Miracle

In a world full of jealousy, where people can't see other's happiness,
getting a supportive pure love in life is truely a miracle,
In a world full of cruelty, where everyone looks for his benefits,
having a helping and selfless heart is a miracle,
In a world full of lies, where people always prefer to wear a mask,
getting someone genuinely trustworthy is a miracle,
In a world full of hatred, where being competitive is now on trend,
having an encouraging partner is truely a miracle,
In a dirty mud where no one even wants to walk around for a while,
Emergence of a beautiful smiling lotus flower is a miracle,
In a world full of restrictions, where people have their own limits,
Birds flying freely high in the sky is truely a miracle,
In a garden, melody being sung by a black cuckoo is a miracle,
The sea holding millions of lifes and giving birth to pearls is a miracle,
In a world where we pay a lot of money for getting lights at night,
Light of the stars so far away, peeping into our eyes so easily is a miracle,
This universe never cease to amaze us with all of it's miracles,
The moment you believe in it's magic, even your existence will look like a miracle!!!

तब क्या तुम मेरी हो जाओगी ?

बुन- बुन कर सारी उलझनों को
मैं सुलझी सी एक डोरी बनाऊँगा
कौवे के उन काओं- काओं से
कुछ मीठी सी एक धुन बनाऊँगा
एक सूखे से स्तंभ पेड़ पर
कुछ फूलों की लटें लगाऊँगा
तुम कुछ भी बेसुरा सा गुनगुनाना
मैं सुरीला तुम पर एक गीत गाऊंगा
तब क्या तुम मेरी हो जाओगी..?
तुम्हारे मुरझाये से चेहरे पर
रंगों से प्यारी सी मुस्कान बनाऊँगा,
तुम्हारे बिखरे बालों को संभलकर
कुछ प्यारी सी बेख़ौफ़ जुल्फे बनाऊँगा,
तुम्हारी सिसकियों को संज्यो कर
दूर कहीं नदियों में बहाऊंगा,
टूटी हर कांच की चीज़ों को जोड़कर
तुम्हारे लिए एक प्यारी सी आकृति बनाऊँगा,
तुम्हारे आँसुओ के एक- एक कतरे को
एक कांच की बोतल में कैद कर
अपने सपनो की छोटी सी नाव तैराउंगा
इस अंधकार सी दुनियाँ में
तुम्हारे लिए आसमान में ,अपने ब्रश से
खूबसूरत से बादल बनाऊँगा
हेयर ड्रायर से तुम्हारी जुल्फ़े उड़ाऊंगा
तुम्हे काजल लगाऊँगा
ये जो दो पेड़ है

इनमे झूला बांध
तुम्हें झूला झुलाऊंगा
हर गीत तुम संग गाऊंगा
हर नींद तुम संग
हर ख्वाब में तुम्हें ही लाऊँगा
तुम्हे फूलों से नहलाऊंगा
तुम्हारी मुस्कुराती तस्वीरें बनाऊँगा
सर्दियों में तुम्हे गले लगाऊँगा
और तुम सा ही होजाऊँगा

तब क्या तुम मेरी हो जाओगी..?

जन्मदिन

तारीख़ 19 सितम्बर 2019,
आज से ठीक एक साल पहले की बात है
मैं आधे नशे में, कुछ ख़ास दोस्तों के मुस्कुराते चेहरे और सामने एक बड़ा सा केक, ढ़ेर सारे फ़ोन कॉल और बधाई के संदेश , मेरे एक हाथ में फ़ोन और दूसरे हाथ से केक काटता मैं, एक - एक कर मैं भी , लोगों के अनुसार लोगों हो एक छोटा सा thankyou बोलता, कोई emoji भेजता, तो मैं भी thankyou के साथ एक इमोजी लगता और भेज देता, की अचानक एक massage सामने आया
लिखा था कि,
"जन्मदिन की ढ़ेर सारी शुभकामनाएं, मैं तुमसे बेहद प्यार करती हूँ, मैं तुम्हारे सारे सपनें पूरे होने की कामना करती हूँ, भगवान तुम्हें खुश रखे तुम और भी ज्यादा ख़ुशियों के हक़दार हो, जो भी परेशानियाँ हो जब भी तुम्हे जरूरत हो मैं हमेशा तुम्हारे साथ रहूँगी, मैं ख़ुदको खुशनसीब मानती हूँ, जो तुम मुझे मिले, मेरी ज़िन्दगी का हिस्सा बनने के लिए शुक्रिया, ये जन्मदिन तुम्हारी ज़िन्दगी में ढेर सारी खुशियाँ लेकर आये, फिर एक बार जन्मदिन मुबारक हो,

एक साल हो गया, वक़्त के साथ सारी बातें फ़ीकी पड़ गयीं, वो शख्स अब नही है,
शायद यह संदेश किसी और को भी देने गया होगा, फिलहाल वो जहाँ भी हो, कुशल हो !

तुम्हारा शहर

उससे बिछड़े कई साल हो गए
पर आज भी वो मेरे दिल के किसी कोने में
छिपी बैठी है, और वक़्त बेवक़्त
मेरे न चाहते हुए भी
झलक आती है,
कभी मेरी बातों से तो
कभी बेवजह मेरी आँखों से
लोग कई बार कहते हैं कि
भूल जा उसे
और मैं हर बार मुस्कुरा कर यही कहता हूँ
क्यूँ भूल जाऊं..?
भूलना जरूरी है क्या..!

मैं किसी ट्रैन के सफ़र में था
स्लीपर क्लास, लोअर बर्थ
और मेरे कानों में बड़े-बड़े हेडफोन्स
हेडफोन्स इसलिए नहीं
की मुझे गाने सुनने का शौक है
बल्कि मैं तो हेडफोन्स इसलिए लगाता हूँ
की ये मुझे बाहर की दुनियाँ से काटे रखते हैं
हाँ वही दुनियाँ
जिसे मैं पिछले कई सालों से नज़रअंदाज़ करता आ रहा हूँ

रात का सफ़र था, ट्रैन भी चल पड़ी
चलती हुई ट्रैन में सोना मुझे
माँ और नानी की गोद की याद दिलाते हैं
शायद यह भी कारण होगा की,
ट्रैन में मेरी नींद लगते, देर नहीं लगती

एकाएक मेरी आँख खुली,
ट्रैन किसी स्टेशन पर रुकी थी
ट्रैन की आधी खुली खिड़की से धूप झाक रही थी
मैं खिड़की पूरी खोल दिया,
देखा तो ये शहर तुम्हारा था
फिर एक बार तुम्हारे शहर के कितने करीब
फिर एक बार तुम्हारे इस अनजान शहर में
कहीं खुद को ढूंढता मैं,

वही पुराना स्टेशन , गर्मा- गरम चाय की केतली
और मेरे पसंदीदा समोसे
सारी चीज़ों को नज़रअंदाज़ कर
चंद मिनटों तक मेरी आँखें उसी को ढूंढती रही
वो नज़र न आई , कहीं भी नहीं
मैंने अपनी नज़रें दौड़ाकर स्टेशन का हर कोना देखा
प्लेटफॉर्म नंबर 1,2,3
ब्रिज के ऊपर , समोसे के स्टाल पर
वो नज़र न आई
कहीं भी नहीं
ट्रैन चलने को थी

ट्रैन की रफ्तार में मुझसे बिछडती वो
और उसका खूबसूरत शहर...

मैं और ग़ुम - सुम

बाक़ी दिनों से ये दिन कुछ खास था, दिन नागपंचमी, और हिन्दू धर्म में ये दिन कुछ खास अहिमियात रखता है,

नागपंचमी हम हिन्दू अपने पहले त्यौहार के रूप में मनाते है,
घर में पूजा होती है, साथ ही साथ स्वादिष्ट पकवान भी बनते हैं,
पर इन सबके परे, मुझे ये दिन याद है क्योंकि इस दिन मेरी ग़ुम-सुम से मुलाकात हुई,
हाँ, 【ग़ुम-सुम】 बिल्ली के दो छोटे-छोटे बच्चे , बड़ी ही मासूमियत से भरे दो चेहरे,
मैं काफ़ी देर तक उन्हें देखता रहा, थोड़ा खुद डरा, थोड़ा उन्हें डराया, पर वे तो बड़े बहादुर थे, बिल्कुल नहीं डरे
मैंने उनपर तरस खाकर, उनके सामने दूध से भरी एक कटोरी रख दी,
वे बहुत ही जल्द सारा दूध पी गए, मैं थोड़ी देर कुछ सोचा फिर उनका नाम 【 ग़ुम-सुम】 रख दिया, साथ ही साथ अपने instagram और whatsapp पर एक स्टोरी शेयर किया..

Story थी कि,
ये दोनों सुबह से आगये हैं आज, सुबह से मेरे ही बगीचे में हैं , इनका नाम मैं 【 ग़ुम-सुम】 रख दिया हूँ, और एक लीटर दूध पिला दिया हूँ, जल्दी-जल्दी पी गए हैं और इसी कारण मेरे घरवाले मुझे आज शाम की चाय नहीं देंगे, अगर कल भी यहीं रहे, तो इनके लिए बगीचे में ही छोटा सा घर बनवा दूँगा,
ठीक किया हूँ बताओ...?

स्टोरी शेयर करते ही, लोगों के तरह- तरह के रिप्लाई आने लगे, जिसमे , क्या खूब भाई, बहुत ही बढ़िया, और क्या बात है शामिल थे।

मुझे 【गुम-सुम】 की तस्वीरें लेना बेहद पसंद था और जायज भी था , आखिर किसे पसंद न होता ,
वो दो मासूम से बच्चे कभी पूरे बगीचे में खेलते , कभी थक कर एक दूसरे के ऊपर अपने नन्हें- नन्हें पैर रख सो जाते और दूध दो तो झटपट पी जाते,
और मैं उन्हें देखता रहता,
आख़िरकार मैंने उनके लिए एक छोटा सा , टीन का घर बनवा ही दिया, पर उसमे कोई दरवाजा नहीं लगवाया
कारण था कि , मुझे किसी को भी कैद करना बिलकुल भी पसंद नहीं,

यकीन मानो ढ़ेर सारे पछी रहते हैं मेरे बगीचे में, जो कि समय- समय पर खाना खाने और पानी पीने आते हैं, जिन्हें मैने कैद नहीं किया हैं वो आज़ाद हैं ठीक मेरे और आपकी तरह,
और अब 【गुम-सुम】 भी उनमें से एक ,
【गुम-सुम】 मेरे दिल के बेहद क़रीब ,

हमारे घर में दूध वाला सुबह 8 बजे आता है, मैं हर रोज़ सुबह दूध लेने लगा, और हर रोज़ दूधवाले से कहता
"भईया थोड़ा जल्दी आया करो 【गुम-सुम】 को भूख लगी होती है"
घर में चाय बनने से पहले , मैं गुम-सुम को गुम-सुम की कटोरी में दूध दे आता, और गुम-सुम भी बड़े मज़े से दूध पीने लगती,
काफ़ी दिनों तक ये सिलसिला चलता रहा
कई दिनों तक 【गुम-सुम】 मेरे बगीचे में ऐसे रही , की मानो ये उसी का घर हो,

एक दिन मैं सुबह जल्दी उठ गया, दिन रविवार , घर में सभी लोग सो रहे थे, बगीचे में जाकर देखा तो
【गुम-सुम】 अपने घर में नहीं थी, मैंने गुम-सुम को काफ़ी देर तक और काफ़ी दिनों तक खोजा, 【गुम-सुम】 कहीं न मिली,

मैंने गुम-सुम का घर नहीं हटाया , और उसके दूध पीने की कटोरी उसी जगह पर पलट कर रख दिया,
कि 【गुम-सुम】 कभी आएगी तो रहेगी,

इसलिए अब मैं हर रोज़ दूध लेता हूँ, और हर रोज़ दूधवाले भईया से कहता हूँ कि " भईया थोड़ी जल्दी आया करो" पर अब ये नहीं कहता
कि 【गुम-सुम】 को भूख लगी होगी,
क्योंकि 【गुम-सुम】 तो जा चुकी हैं।

और वो चली गई

बारिश जैसे होने को थी
खुशियाँ सारी खोने को थी
गम के बादल जैसे छा रहे थे
हर पत्ते मुरझा रहे थे
मुझे छोड़ बाकी सबको ये खबर थी
वो भी थोड़ी बेसबर थी
मै भी बस कहने को था
हर गम अभी सहने को था
कहना था ठहर जा
बस इस बार मुझमे यूँ बिखर जा
सारे गम भुला दे
मेरी इस मोहब्बत को
अपने दिल में जगह दे
उसने भी खुद को संभाल के रखा था
अब और नहीं रहना तुम्हारे साथ
बस ये ही कहा था
उसने हाल खुद का
अपनी आँखों से कहा था
बेबस मै बँधी हुई
और ना जाने क्या-क्या कहा था
अचानक
बारिश सी होने लगी थी
खुशियाँ सारी खोने लगी थी
गम के बादल छा गए
पत्ते सारे मुरझा गए
मैंने भी उसके फैसले को गले लगाया
बिना क्यूँ - क्या पूछे
तुझे समझता हूँ

उसको ये एहसास दिलाया..
और...
और वो चली गई
मेरी हँसी, मेरी ख़ुशी,
उसकी हसीं उसकी खुशी
अधूरे सपने और
ढ़ेर सारी यादें देकर,

आख़री मुलाकात

आज भी तुम,
कई दफा मेरे ख़्वाबों में आ जाती हो
तुम्हारी लम्बी - लम्बी दो गुथी चोटी
बालों में सफ़ेद रंग का रिबन
तुम्हारे फूले - फूले गाल
वही तुम्हारा स्कूल का सलवार सूट
और प्रेस की हुई चुनरी
हाथ में पानी की बोतल
और रुमाल,
आज भी क्या तुम वैसी ही दिखती हो
क्यूँ की उसके बाद कभी मुलाक़ात ही ना हुई

याद है तुम्हे..?
तुम शहर के एक छोर और मै दूसरी छोर में रहता था
ना चाहते हुए भी हमारी स्कूल बस अलग थीं
मै 4 और तुम 5 नंबर बस से जाती थी
कैसे मै अपना बैग अपनी बस में रख कर
तुम्हारी बस के पास आकर खड़ा हो जाता था..

आज भी क्या इंसान के दिखने तक
खिड़की से bye..! करती हो तुम..?
दे देती हो क्या अब भी रुमाल अपना
किसी को भी जैसे,
बेवज़ह मुझे दे जाया करती थी
आँखों में अब भी क्या काजल लगाती..?
ठीक वैसे ही जैसे उस वक़्त लगाया करती थी

क्या सच में अब भी वैसी ही दिखती हो तुम

जैसे मेरे ख्वाब में आती हो

क्यूँ की उसके बाद कभी मुलाक़ात ही न हुई..

जवाब "तुम्हारे आख़री ख़त का"

किसी रोज़ किसी ने पूछा था मुझसे की
"डरते हो अब भी मोहब्बत करने से या ख़याल मेरा जाता नहीं"

हाँ अब नहीं होती किसी से मोहब्बत
न शख्स से, न जिस्म से
न किसी के हाथों से, न ही किसी के आँखों से
न किसी की हंसी से, न ज़ुल्फो से
और न ही किसी की रूह से..
न ही किसी के ख़्वाबों में जाने की मोहब्बत
न ही किसी को ख़्वाबों में लाने की मोहब्बत
न किसी को पाने की मोहब्बत
न ही डर किसी के खो जाने का..
न खुद से मोहब्बत
न ही तुझसे मोहब्बत

मोहोब्बत है तेरे ज़िक्र से
अपनी शायरियों से
अपने काम से
अपने नाम से
तेरे धोखा देने से
उन खोखलों वादों से
तेरी झूठी हसीं से
मेरे महकते ख्वाबों से
उन लम्हों से

इन दूरियो से
जो रोक रखी अब तक मुझको
इन लोहे की ज़ंजीरो से

और उस शहर से
जहाँ मै लौट के वापस जा न सका
जहाँ का हर कोना
मुझे तेरे होने का एहसास दिलाते हैं !

रातें स्कूल की यादें

सो भी जाओ
क्यों अब तक जाग रहे हो
सारी दुनियाँ तो भाग ही रही है
उसी रास्ते क्यों तुम भी भाग रहे हो

याद करो वो भारी बस्ता
जिसको काँधे पे ढोया था
सिखा दिया क्या उसने सब कुछ
फिर क्यों इतना कुछ खोया था
याद करो जब रोते रोते
घर को लौटा करते थे
ABCD अल्फा, गामा
और थीटा थीटा करते थे
याद करो वो पहली लड़की
जो तुम्हे देख मुस्काई थी
उससे भी था कुछ कहना
पर सिर पर बहुत पढ़ाई थी
खत्म होगया अब वो किस्सा
बचपन जिसको कहते थे
माथे पर न शिकन ज़रा सी
और मस्ति में तुम रहते थे

किस सोच में डूबे हो अब तक
ख्वाबों में कहीं खो भी जाओ
रात भी काफी होगई अब तो
तारों तले अब सो भी जाओ।

खामोशियाँ

तुम ख़ामोश सी
मैं ख़ामोश सा
सारे शख़्स , ये रास्ते
सारी उम्मीदें , सारे वादे
मेरे शब्द, हमारे जज़्बात
सभी आहिस्ता ख़ामोश होगये हैं
मैं फ़िर एक दफ़ा डूबता जा रहा हूँ
और एक दफ़ा फिर
सब ख़ामोश देख रहें है
ना जाने कैसी ये खामोशी है
ना मैं कुछ कहता हूँ
ना कोई सुनता है
बस ये खोमोशियाँ हैं
जो बस चीख़ती रहतीं हैं।

टूटती उम्मीदें

वो शख़्स जिसे तुम मिली थी
एक उम्मीद बनकर,
वो फिर कहीं खोने लगा है
एक दफ़ा फिर सीने में
एक हल्का सा दर्द होने लगा है
कुछ गाने सुनते ही
फिर नम होने लगीं हैं ये आँखे
फिर लोगों से छुप कर
वो शख़्स कहीं रोने लगा है
सुबह पसंद नहीं अब उसे
सारा दिन बेमकसद फिर सोने लगा है
और ना जाने !
क्या तलाशती रहतीं है उसकी निगाहें
ना जाने कौन सा नया ख़्वाब पिरोने लगा है
तस्वीरें तुम्हारी अब तक हैं उसके पास
उन्हें सिरहाने रख सोने लगा है
तुम्हारे जाने से वो शख़्स
फिर एक दफ़ा खोने लगा है

इक्चामृत्यु { Euthanasia}

आपमें से कई सारे लोग मुझे जानते होंगे, आप मे से कई लोग को ये भी लगता होगी कि मैं आपसे बात नही करना चाहता या मेरे कुछ खास दोस्त हैं या मैं सिर्फ उनसे ही बात करना पसंद करता हूँ, दरअसल मेरी किसी से भी बात नहीं होती, मुझे नहीं पता आपको ये महसूस होता है या नहीं, जिंदिगी में एक समय आता है जब इंसान को लगता है कि सब कुछ छोड़ कर कहीं दूर चले जाना चाहिए , हाँ मेरा मतलब आत्महत्या से है, पर इसे आत्महत्या नहीं कह सकते क्योंकि आत्महत्या की कोई वजह होती है , ये कुछ बेवज़ह सा है

लोग इसे इक्चामृत्यु कहते हैं और मुझे ये ख्याल हर रोज़ आता है,

हो सकता है मुझे किसी (pyschologist) मनोचिकित्सक की जरूरत हो

कई बार मैं कोशिश भी किया हूँ लोगों को समक्ष ये अजीब सी ख्वाइश रखने की पर कुछ हुआ नहीं, कोई खास वज़ह नहीं है कि मैं ये प्रयत्न करूँ, बस कुछ अधूरा सा लगता है, पैसा , घर , माँ-बाप , गाड़ी सब है , हुनर भी है, हाल में ही मेरे एक बुक पब्लिश हुई, "अनकहीं बातें" थोड़ा देर खुश था , फिर वही उदासी,

2 साल पहले की बात है मै ग्वालियर में 10th floor अपने फ्लैट no. 8387 में बालकनी से पैर लटका कर दारू पी रहा था, ख़याल आया कि मर जाना चाहिए, पूरा माइंड सेट , की बहुत तेज़ सू-सू आगई , मुझे लगा कि आखरी बार कर के मरना ठीक रहेगा, वापस आया तो वो मोममेन्ट जा चुका था, फिर मेरा मन नहीं किया

वो पल चला गया,

आज भी कुछ ऐसा ही हुआ , मैं ब्रिज के ऊपर खड़ा था, लगा मर जाना चाहिए , हल्की-हल्की बारिश हो रही थी , मैं सिगरेट जलाया और ब्रिज की दीवार पर खड़ा होगया, अचानक पानी की एक बूंद ने मेरी सिगरेट बुझा दी,

मैं सिगरेट जलाने नीचे उतरा , तो फिर से वो पल जा चुका था , खैर

फ़िलहाल अभी ज़िंदा हूँ, जब तक हूँ ऐसे ही लिखता रहूँगा,

आप पढ़ते रहिएगा।

एक सफ़र में !

शायद मिलेगा मौका मुझे किसी एक दिन सफर में निकलने का, वो सफर जहां रास्ते अनजान होंगे, जहां की गलियां मुझे देख कर जानने की कोशिश करेंगी "वो लड़की कौन है? कहां से आयी हैं वो लड़की जिसका रंग ज़रा सांवला है?"
एक ऐसी जगह जहां लोग मुझे पहचानते ना होंगे लेकिन मुझे देखते ही उनके चेहरे पर मुस्कान जरूर आएगी ।वो महफ़ूज़ सफ़र जिसमें मंजिल को पहुंचने की जल्दी नहीं होगी, ना सफर पूरा करने की हड़बड़ी, ना ही होगा लौट कर वापस घर आने का कोई इरादा ।सफ़र जहां रात होते ही मैं तलाश करूंगी एक छत मगर सो जाऊंगी खुले आसमान के नीचे चैन कि नींद, बिना किसी फिकर के ।ना होगा समान ज्यादा - ना कोई ज्यादा बोझा होगा, मुझे चिंता ना होगी कि मैनें क्या पहना है, मुझे अफ़सोस नहीं होगा मेरे अकेले होने से और फिर शायद मिलेगा मुझे मौका किसी दिन एक सफ़र में निकलने का ।

Ashwini Prasad

My First Love Affair

When I passed my 10th std I went to junior college and took admission in 11th std science subject there I met lot of students but 3 or five students became my friend one name is Priya Thomas, Sony mekapogu, Kumari Sualaja Smita Yadav and me we became friends we talked about everything food love travel mainly about class boys during my teenage years I had crush on one south actor actor his name is Prithiviraj that time I heard news he was getting married so we were talking about another boys one of my friend Sualaja she told she had boyfriend in Kerala and she is dating and another friend Priya also had a boyfriend of his own religion and Sony had crush on south actor Prabhas we were happy with our friendship as the year passed by we reached 12th std and 12th also complete I was very in physics and my practical was also not good as the board exam result came everyone passed I failed in physics subject rest I got all the subject my friend went for graduation I repeat ed my exam but did not pass so finally I decided to take commerce as subject in 12th then I passed I am now in ty BCom

Baisakhi Das

Loved you

Loved you,
The second I saw your face,
Just haven't met you yet,
It was love at first sight
I knew we were gonna stick like glue
It must have been a miracle
Waiting for years,
Never knew help could come so fast,
I was lonely,
Back in that dark alley,
Helplessly laying like a freak,
You were glowingly hot!
Like my sun,
My militia,
You gave hope,
Carried me on and off,
Driven me to the nearest hospital,
I pretended to be unconscious,
I could feel your kiss,
Touching mine,
Like a lovely weather,
Passing grand Central station nearby,
Just haven't met you yet,
Not personally,
Not physically,
But you were there,
Loved you like a child,
You were my babe,
I was your prince,
We were in love,

Hope you come back soon,
Maybe give me your final kiss,
A lovely hug,
A passionate one,
No,
Just a Friendship bonding..
Maybe.
Just a help
Hope you like it!!!

Chetan Bansor

"फ़क़ीर सी लगती है"

देख कर अनदेखा कर रहा हूं आजकल
मेरी कश्मकश दीवार पर टंगी तस्वीर सी लगती है

किसे सुनाऊं ये हालात ए दिल इस महफ़िल में
हर किसी की फितरत तो यहां एक सी लगती है

सुनना कौन चाहेगा किसी की तन्हाइयों के किस्से
यहां हर किसी की कहानी शोर सी लगती है

दीवाना कहे कोई या आशिक़ ही कह ले
हर रांझे को तलाश यहां उसकी हीर की लगती है

फिर दीवारों में कैद हो जाना भी मंज़ूर होगा
गर इज़हार ए मोहब्बत सलीम सी लगती है

हर कोई आग में जलकर बस राख ही हुआ था
शमा के साथ जलना परवाने की रीत सी लगती है

कोई कह दे मुझे तुझे इश्क़ ना हो कभी
आजकल ये बददुआ भी मुझे दुआ सी लगती है

अंधेरों में ढूंढ लेता था जो शख्स कभी
दिन के उजालों में भी उसकी आँखे बंद सी लगती है

जिसे परवाह नहीं गम ए ज़माने की देखो

चमत्कार

मुद्दत लग गये तुम्हें अपनाने
ओर कौई मिल गई,
कर रहे थे प्यार तुम्हें कैसे
ओर कौई मिल गई ?
चमत्कार होगा कोयला ढूढते
हीरा ढूंढ लिये,
कबतक तुम्हारे पिछे पडते तुम

God's Words Matters

Dear Grief,
It seems that you are standalone and my inseparable mate. I wanted to leave you, come out from your grip but no I was wrong, you are my soul mate I can feel that. You have chosen me when I was betrayed by the most trusted person.
But friend, sometimes if you wish you can roam freely and stay alone but I know, you also need a shoulder to lean on or a bear hug to embrace and thus you have chosen me. Dear Grief, yesterday I was praying to God and requested Him to do a miracle in my life and help me to see the brighter side of the world around me.
God said, 'I will.' So, my mate, I believe you have to look for a new home to dwell in. God's words matter and believe me I will remember you always.
Yours truly.

Life Without Love Is Like

Life without love is like
Heart without heartbeat,
Life without friends is like
Night without moon,
Life without seasons is like
Week without weekend,
Life without problems is like
Beauty without smile...

Disita Sikdar

Amidst the Sky

Rusted from the last night rain
I waited for the sun to rise,
Washed over in grass and muted blues until the sky finally caught fire !

Light kissed the edges of clouds
Everything bathed in shades of amber.

Standing beside the window
I tried catching the skies with my eyes.
The splendid and endless world to touch.

The moon could be seen again flickering amid stardust.
The moon followed that path again, the known address to the never-ending space in between my contemplation and then,
Slowly the moonlight passed through caressing my soul and with brush strokes painted the canvas of the sky,
and I woke up again
With wings to fly.

Miracles Are Like Magic!

Miracles!
Miracles are like magic!
When ever they happen it surprises you.
Miracles are like magic!
When ever they happen it is as if
there is no other like them.
Miracles are like magic!
You look at them with awe, as you let
your jaw drop.
Miracles are like magic!
They are gorgeous things.
Miracles are like magic!
When they happen, you would
become flabbergasted.
Miracles are like magic!
It would seem as if you cannot live
without them.
Well, what to say?
'Miracles are magical!'

औरत

वो एक औरत है,
समंदर जैसी शांति है उसमें
परंतु समय आने पर,
समंदर में भी.....
तूफान आ जाया करता है.......

Life

मैं हर दिन उठता अपने सपनों के लिए
पर सपने साकार दूसरों के किए
वो कहते थे कि हाथ मत छोड़ना....
आप बहुत ज़रूरी हो मेरे लिए...
उनके सपने क्या पूरे हुए वो चल दिए हाथों में हाथ किसी और का लिए...
दिन निकलते गए शाम ढलती गई
कभी तो जीवन में नया सवेरा हो
मैं हमेशा कहता रहा ये आपका है वो आपका है....
कभी तो कुछ हमारा भी हो।
प्यार बहुत करता होगा तुझसे
इसीलिए तेरा बुरा नहीं चाहता होगा...
मत कर इतने कठोर शब्दों का प्रयोग दिल उसका भी दुःख ता होगा......
गर सज़ा होती अच्छे इंसान होने की, तो इस गुनाह के लिए
उसे दर्ज़नो बार फांसी पे लटका चुका होता
ना लेना किसिका उपकार, समझेंगे तुझे लाचार
ना बनना सलाहकार, समझेंगे तुझे बेकार
ना होना इतना दिलदार, की दिल टूटे तेरा बार बार
अपने लिए कुछ करना सीख तभी सपने तेरे होंगे साकार

Rape

She encircled with customs
Engulfed woh false belief
Giving best to friends family soulmate
Bonded by walls hiding over all
Engorged by creepe hands evil eyes
Snatching the innocence
Ravish the self respect
Shouting soul she was
Painful body broken soul bleeds around
Hoping eyes to saviours
Defloration of budded flower
Neither one nor two shamed to be count
Customs beliefs thoughts sailing nightmares
A friend now corners wiping the eyes
Determine again she redecorate the soul brighten upto the blue roof high again

Unconditional Friendship

No, we don't belong to same blood
nor we have similar ideas of friendships,
More than best friends
We two are soul mates,
We don't bother about
what we get from each other,
We don't bother about
what we personally go through,
We're there for each other though
whenever and wherever it's needed,
Providing emotional ventilation to each other
And being warmth in each other's humid days
We built our bond the strongest as stone,
Being rare for each other and peculiar in connection,
we passed all the tough levels of friendships,
We respect each other's differences
And we enhance each other's growth,
We accept each other's flaws
And adapt each other's qualities
And that's how we proved our friendship as the unique and
unconditional one.

Eshika Kumari

Death is the ultimate conclusion of dramatized life.
Light cannot shine under the Sun.
जब मुसीबतों का पहाड़ टूट पड़ता है न,
तो ग़म भी महसूस करने की फुरसत रब नहीं देता ।।

बुलाती थी मगर जाने का नहीं था न, राहत साहब।।।

खुबसूरती सिर्फ एक दिखावा है।
आंखों का धोखा और,
नज़रों का फरेब है।
जो समझ जाए वो होशियार और
जो न समझे वो बेवकूफ।
नैनो से तकरार और,
जिस्म से प्यार।
यही तो है हुस्न का उल्फत-ऐ-अंदाज।

You have offered the best uncomfortable sofa where I can take the nap of my death.....

E Pavithra

Mirror

Trapped in a Maze,
With people's cunning gaze....
I was swayed to fit myself
Into their mindset,
But,
Here am combating with
My own mental state.......
I was smeared as "liar"
But,
I am struggling with my inner fear...
Soon,
I realised, Iam a puppet
for own my story with someone's script!!!
Trapped in a pool,
Sinking all the time with no soul...
Tried to shut my mouth,
So one hears me sob
And,
There was a person ,
Who was ready to mop....
Thought there is no one,
Who could travel through darkness..
But,
I was such an oblivious
Who is unwitting of her selfness.....
Oh! It is the person in the mirror
Of whom I was unaware......
You can't be yourself
When people rule you around,
Being infuriated, I have no go,

But leave you wound...
You were there from my first breathe,
So you would till the last, I am vexed
As,
I still couldn't clear the cataract in mind
To discover you, coz I am too perplexed!!!!
So,
Let me accept my mistakes,
Let me accept my past,
Let me accept my shadows,
And attain Self-individuation
By resisting the norms created ny people......
Coz,
The person in the mirror,
Will never leave me forever!!!!

Gorang Choubisa

टूटे अल्फ़ाज़

इश्क़ की जमीं पर सज़दे हज़ार देख लिए,
प्यार में लोगों के दर्द,मरते हज़ार देख लिए,

जिस्म की तड़प में कोई मरता आज तक ना देखा,
रूह से मरते जज़्बात आज देख लिए।।

शामिल नहो हो सकता कोई इस सजदे में,
बेदर्द महोब्बत में आशिक़ हज़ार देख लिए,

तुम क्यूं रूठते हो इस बेरंग सी दुनिया से,
लोगों ने भी अपने रंग हज़ार देख लिए ,

और वो आशिक़ मरता तो क्या ना करता,
उसने भी काफिरों के सज़दे हजार देख लिए,

मिट्टी से बंधे रूह के लोगों में भी,
रूह के टकराव हज़ार देख लिए,

उसने इस मासूम सी शक्ल में छिपे,
आस्तीनों के शैतान हज़ार देख लिए,

तुम्हारे चाहने से वो फिर लौट ना आएगा,
ख़ुद की बिगड़न में उसने,दर्द हज़ार भर दिए।।

वो बड़ा इतराता था उगते सूरज की रोशनी में,
किसी की बिछड़न ने, अंधेरे हज़ार कर दिए,

औऱ अब तक वो लौटा क्यूं नहीं इस आस में,
स्याही से लफ़्ज़ों ने दर्द, हज़ार भर दिए।।

Note to Self

Never lose yourself for someone ,
If they're okay with losing you,
Life is too short ,keep no regrets
Take your lessons and keep moving on,
Keep always a part of you for yourself,
Just find your worth within yourself, make them crave your vibes,
Never loathe and question your existence,
If they ridicule you for not living upto their expectations,
Never remain stuck in the memory lane of past,
Consider that as your strength for stepping into a new world,
You deserve equal respect and love,
Never beg for something that is already yours,
Its okay to feel things to depths and love people intensely and unintentionally,
For that is always a blessing in disguise which is hard to find,
Stay positive and keep trying,
Good things will happen soon ,just wait for the right moment ,
You just need to remind yourself of what you have lived and overcomed.

Changing one own self – Real Miracle

The only real valuable thing is intuition and the only source of knowledge is experience.
Albert Einstein…
Intuition when nourished by physical and mental involvement results in to experience and experience gives the real knowledge and knowledge based on experience brings positive changes in a person. So it can be claimed that changing one own self is the real miracle. It is worth notable in this regard that change comes from within.
On the other hand the miracles what we read in our holy scriptures are extraordinary events that are not explicable by natural or scientific laws and is therefore attributed to a divine and celestial beings. To experience them one requires a level of innocence, purity of mind, devotion and surrender to divine which again is possible if we bring the required changes within ourselves. So if we can start practicing changing ourselves as per the situation, start learning compromising and start accepting the will of divine then in long run we may be able to see miracles what today we have accepted in the form of beliefs.

Positivity Brings Success

Think an idea,
To start
Create a process,
To execute
Work with endurance,
To proceed
Soul with positiveness,
To succeed.

Gayathri. S

Voice Of Colours

Our life is filled with various types of emotions. According to me "if emotions are not there life is useless”. There is always a strong bonding between colours and emotions. Colours are the reflection of emotions. Here I have shared my imagination story in the concept of voice of colours Once upon a time there was a village called "Red village” This village is filled by one and only one colour that is "Red”. Red colour represents "Angry / Danger”. The people's in the village is also red as I mentioned above red reflect the angry emotion so they are in angry always. we have to make proper use of it. God created every tiny thing with a cause. We human being are created to exhibits our talents and if we exhibit our talents in a proper way surely, we will get a Blooms in our life. So the trespassers get afraid to get into the village. One fine day ! There was a magic painter who like to be everything in colourful he used his "Rainbow Mat” for travelling accidentally he came across the "Red village' and get shocked because of the colour "Red". According to the painter the red colour brings bad vibration so the painter would like to change the Red village into colourful village. The Magic painter spoke with everyone and he conveyed about the colour Red and their vibration. At, first The Magic painter change the colour of Plant. The Magic painter decide to give a green colour for then. The reason behind of choosing the green colour is to represent the "Healing therapy" to all.so only whenever we see the colour green plants our pains are healed and as a result, we are receiving the fresh air them. Plants act as a remedy for our pain so deforestation should be avoided. Next, some food items came forward to change the colour for them. The Magic painter gave yellow colour for them because the colour yellow stands for "Energy”. We have to eat healthy food and we have to do regular workouts to stay energy always. Next, Clouds came forward to change the colour for them. The Magic painter decided to give white colour for them because white colour stands for "Cleanliness". Our Mind, Body, Soul should always be very clean. To say that truth the Magic painter gave white colour to the

clouds. Next, Sky came forward to change the colour. The Magic painter decided to give blue colour for them. The colour blue represents "Patience". The sky is very high even though it's very high it remains patience likewise we have to be very patience till we reach our goal. After reaching also we have to be stay calm. Patience results always good. To say that truth the Magic painter gave blue colour for them. Next, Building came forward to change the colour. The Magic painter gave purple colour for them. The purple colour represents "Ambition". In our life we have to set our Ambition and we have to work hard to achieve our Ambition. This is the secret key for our success. To say that information the Magic painter gave purple colour Next, some dresses came forward to change the colour for them. The Magic painter gave pink colour for them. The pink colour denotes "Love". The Magic painter indirectly says that we have to love each other and that love should be healthy love. We should not hurt others. Always we have to be the giver of love. It makes us happy in our life. By seeing the colour changes in Red village automatically the mind set of people begins to change. Their pains are healed, they receive the energy from foods, they learned about cleanliness and their results, they learned how to stay patience even in very critical situations, they set a strong full ambition and learned how to work hard, love arises each and everyone's heart. And it's the time to revel the secret of that Magic painter who travelled with us for a short time he is none other than "GOD". God created everything for a reason. Even the colours speak a lot n work a lot in our emotions why our human being can't do. The life which we are living is a God's gift we have to make a proper use out of it. God doesn't create even a small thing useless. We human beings are created to exhibits our talents to get a blooming life.

What is the Colour?

Colour is the way of exploration. "The soul becomes dyed with the colour of its thought", Marcus Aurelius philosopher. Colours tell us the unknown stories to us which delight not only our eyes but also our mind. It can irritate or soothe your eyes, raise your blood pressure, or suppress your appetite.

A blind person also sees a colour. Which is unpleasant to most of our eyes. It's a way of conveying emotion. Not all colours are unpleasant some help us to overcome the difficulty. Red the colour of human blood, a warrior, is said to be the strongest if he has ensanguined the redness of blood.

Mother nature accommodates the most beautiful colours of life, from black to white and the most beautiful green which reflects growth, vitality, fertility, and harmony. Colour accumulates the way of living life, as a powerful form of communication, colour is just irreplaceable.

चमत्कार...

बात २८ साल पुरानी है। मेरे दादाजी अपने मित्र मण्डल के साथ अमरनाथ की यात्रा पर गए थे। उनकी मंडली २० लोगों की थी। मेरे दादाजी की उम्र कुछ ६८ साल रही होगी।
वे लोग बाबा बर्फानी के दर्शन कर के लौट रहे थे तभी अचानक न जाने कैसे दादाजी अपनी मंडळी से बिछड़ गए। उन्होंने चारों तरफ देखा पर आसपास अपनी मंडळी का कोई नही दिखा। दूसरे लोगों से पूछताछ की पर किसीको कुछ नही पता था। दादाजी थोड़े गभरा गए। फिर कुछ सोच के आगे बढ़े। उन्हें लगा कि थोड़ा आगे बढ़ेंगे तो कोई न कोई तो मिल ही जायेगा।
ऐसा सोच के वे आगे बढ़े लेकिन उन्हें कोई नही मिला। वे थोड़ा परेशान हुए। उस समय में मोबाइल फोन तो थे नही तो संपर्क करना संभव नही था। उन्होंने ने भोलेनाथ को मन ही मन याद किया और आगे बढ़े। कुछ ही कदम चले थे कि पीछे से किसी ने उनका हाथ पकड़ा और अपने साथ खींचने लगे। इस से पहले कि दादाजी कुछ समझ पाते उस साधु ने अपनी उंगली से इशारा करके दादाजी को अपनी मंडळी से मिलवा दिया। दादाजी खुशी के मारे अपनी मंडळी की ओर आगे बढ़े पर फिर उस साधु महात्मा का धन्यवाद करने के लिए पीछे मुड़े तो देखा कि वहाँ तो कोई भी नही था। विस्मय से भरी आँखों में आँसू आ गए। वे कौन थे ? क्या स्वयं महादेव आए थे? इन प्रश्नों के बीच यह चमत्कार अमरनाथ धाम में अमर हो गया।

० गुंजन जोगिया....
(सत्य घटना से प्रेरित)

Hasrat Garg

Easy Enough

Miracle (ˈमिरक्ल्)
Noun
1. a wonderful event that seems impossible and that is believed to be caused by God.
(दैवीय घटना, चमत्कार (जिसका कर्ता स्वयं ईश्वर या किसी देवता को माना जाता है)

2. a lucky thing that happens that you did not expect was possible. (आशा या सोच के विपरीत घटी) शुभ घटना,

Oxford dictionary explains miracle in a miraculous way, but the little philosopher in my head says,

"MIRACLE WILL BE WHEN",

- Your parents don't wake you till 11:00 am.
- Your brother accepts your order to serve you a glass of water without calculating the worksheet of his deeds.
- Your best friend offers you the last piece of pizza slice often.
- Your better half comes with a "man of your dreams" tag.
- Your relatives dissolve their matrimonial business established for your future.
- Society doesn't believe in their so-called norms.
- Every man will show their emotions without worrying about 'Born to be brave' title.
- Every woman will be allowed to enter temples without being discriminated.
- Every child will be authorized for his carrier choices.

• Every mother will be in her home beside her son when she dies.
• An empty road will be no longer hell.
• We all will learn the 'Law of contributions.'

चाहे उसे इश्क कहों या प्यार।

एक ढाई अक्षर का जानलेवा वार,
चाहे उसे इश्क कहों या प्यार ।

चल जाता है दिल पे जैसे कोई तलवार,
चाहे उसे इश्क कहों या प्यार ।

जिसके होते ही, लोग भूल जाते है घर-परिवार,
चाहे उसे इश्क कहों या प्यार ।

जिसके लिए लडेंगे, चाहे सामने हो सारा संसार,
चाहे उसे इश्क कहों या प्यार ।

पता है की होगा बुरा अंजाम,
सबको करना है फिर भी एकबार,
चाहे उसे इश्क कहों या प्यार ।

रिश्ते

दुनिया बहोत अजीब है
जो दूर है वो करीब है
वो ही सबका नसीब है
हर बात की यही रीत बन गई
जिन्दगी थोड़ी अपनी भी प्रीत बन गई
इतेफाक होते है सभी के साथ
भले लोगो की कोई भी हो औकात
फिर भी खेल जाते किसी के जज्बात और हम रह जाते खाली हाथ
इसलिए रखिये दिमागी रिश्तों से दूरी
रखो रिश्ता वही जहा दिल का मिलना हो जरूरी
एहसास का भी हो मोल
और इस तरह बनेगे रिस्ते अनमोल

GDP

Now a days GDP is more familiar word to everyone but majority of people do not understand what is GDP, how it is calculated so in this article I am going to example the same. Gross Domestic Product

(GDP) is the monetary value of all finished goods and services made within a country during a specific period. GDP provides an economic snapshot of a country, used to estimate the size of an economy and growth rate. GDP can be calculated in three ways, using expenditures, production, or incomes.

Written out, the equation for calculating GDP is: GDP = private consumption + gross investment + government investment + government spending + (exports – imports). For the gross domestic product, "gross" means that the GDP measures production regardless of the various uses to which the product can be put.

Drawback:-

While GDP is a useful way to get a sense of the state of an economy, it is by no means a perfect approach. One criticism is that it does not account for activities that are not part of the legalized economy. The proceeds of off-the-books labor, some cash transactions, drug dealing, and more are not factored into GDP.

Jeevitha. S

Unflinching Belief Upon Life!

Although she walked through her darkest days,
She always had a glimmer in her eyes .
She believed in something which was unseen and unheard ,
That one thing was her hope on the whole;
She edified something new in all that she went through,
She became aesthetic on the whole,
Miracle does happen at the end ;
When she rejuvenated her soul through her hope.
There exists the glide of positive vibes ,
She summoned more wisdom and insight.
All her dejections flew away ;
And her eyes once again shimmered with jubilance .
Accepting struggles and proceeding further more,
Her puzzles were solved through her beliefs upon life.

Jyoti kukreja

I Was Born As A

I was born as a daughter
For my parents in need of a son.
They said, "we got a princess"
Without doing any discrimination
That I'm not their Prince.

I was born as a sister
For both of my cousins in family
They said, "we got a sibling"
Without doing any discrimination
That we don't share same parents.

I was born as a grand-daughter
For both of my grand-parents
They said, " we got our heir"
Without doing any discrimination
That I'm not their grand-son
Who will take their generation ahead.

I'm born as a girl
For my beloved family
I say, " I'll be the son of my parents
Grand-son for my grand parents
And a brother for my cousins
Taking care of all of their needs
Without doing any discrimination
That I'm not a boy.

Jata V

Say Me Bon Voyage!

Waking up in the morning made me cringe every time. "I don't want to go to school, Pa?", with tears in my eyes. No, not in kindergarten, it's after high school. I can still taste the bitterness of my childhood and so school life even now. Had to catch three buses, never been before the 1st hour of the school got over. Wearing a uniform that was stitched 4 years before, reaching the highest level of embarrassment just by showing up in the mob. My only friends were social anxiety and philopobia. No matter how hard I try, I still failed in the subjects. Never missed the "Worst Handwriting" award any year. Couldn't afford a sports shoe, "Disappear from the ground if you don't have one!", Coach sulked. "What's the price of that Guitar, uncle?", asking that salesman Kuppu, for the 733309th time. "I can surely go to the gym if my savings reach 1500 rupees!", I beamed with that 145 rupees and 50 paise in my hands.

With these confused parents and with those dutiful teachers dragging me out of the class for not doing homework and stuff...I was puzzled why these people compel me to study unnecessary trash. All I dreamt about is learning music, building up my muscles, and doing online jobs until I reach my goal. I yelled at the parent couple, "Why the hell are you wasting your money on my school fees? I just don't want to go to school anymore. Let me have a Guitar!". "What, did you go nuts?", they replied in a chorus.

At last, my hippity-hoppity school life and my never-seen childhood came to an end with me in the Psychiatry ward. "I'm an adult now! I gotta live myself!". Leaving the house, self-working, going to the gym, buying a Guitar, and making music are all on my itinerary of the way to success.

Kiran Khasiya

तुझमे मुझको पयोगी

जबभी तुम्हे मेरी जरूरत हो मुझे याद कर लेना, में तुम्हे तुम्हारी अंदर ही मिलूंगा,
में तुम्हारी यादों में तुमसे मिलूँगा।

जब भी कोई कठिनाई आये मुझे दिलसे याद कर लेना, में तुम्हारे दिल से तुम्हारा रास्ता बनुगा।

जबभी मायूस हो मेरा नाम लेकर मुस्कुरा देना, में तुम्हारी यादों में बसी हुई हसी बनकर मिलूँगा।

जबभी मेरी याद आये तो खुदसे बात कर लेना, में तुमसे तुम्हारे अल्फाज बनकर बात करुगा।

जबभी कोई कठिन फैसला लेना हो अपने दिल पर हाथ रख देना, में तुम्हारे हर फैसले में तुम्हारे साथ मिलूँगा।

मुझे कहि ढूढने की कोशिश मत करना
मैं तुमसे तुम्हारे अंदर मिलूँगा।
मैं तुमसे तुम्हारे दिल और दिमाग में मिलूँगा।
मेरा खयाल रखना

Kavitha P

It was dark
just like the dark jungle
I was lost in the labyrinth of it

You came as a firefly
with the light all I needed
you held my hand
wrapped your arms around me
I touched your scars and felt the pain

All I saw was your eyes
there, the missed piece of my galaxy

Your crescent smile was my oxygen
your heart beat was a wistful lullaby
I slumbered right there
You held me in your hands

We came out,
I woke up;

I learnt
we, two are a beautiful mess
and
a part of black dwarf!

There, I believed miracles happen!

Kiran Kumari

Let's just be friend's!

On an August day with the waving wind
At half past nine my cell phone pinged
You asked me if 'I could be your friend? '
Well, I said "yes" with a happy heart,
Didn't knew that somethin' was about to start.
The days were passing and we were getting close,
With spending time together a Lovely feeling arose.
Everyday started with your morning text,
And every night ended with a late night call.
Those flower's and greetings you used to send ,
Has made it clear that we aren't just friend's.
Everyday was amazing as if love in air got blend,
And we used to plan being together on weekends.
The story sucesseeding next is little awful to say,
As goods in our life aren't always meant to stay.
Now the week plans changed to months,
Late night calls changed to texts.
But it wasn't your fault neither was mine
As the things between us wasn't so fine.
Busy building up a life, skipping time we used to lend,
Feels no more being your girl or having a boyfriend.
Again the day's were passing, this time taking us apart,
And we nothing to say with just a confused heart.
The love and care was fading, but still we were pretending,
Faking feeling's was so childish and was too offending.
On an August night with the waving wind,
It was midnight when my cellphone pinged.
You said this time "Let's just be friends! "
This was the second time you asked
'to be your friend...'
As that was a start this seems an end.
Time helped me know what these words really meant,
Let's just be friend's is actually "The End! "

Kumari Tripti

Birthday Note

Wherever you are, I hope it is where you always wanted to be,
But is it selfish of me to hope that where you always wanted to be is still somewhere close to me?

It is merely mundane to tell you that I miss you today and every second of every day,
But is it crazy for me to expect, that in some corner of your heart, you too feel this way?

I admit today that listening to your favorite songs or dancing in the rains is not the same anymore (trust me I tried!)
But why does it feel, like every time I watch the moon, if feels like you are gazing right back, just the way you did when we would walk at the shore.

You don't know how much I wish I could just reach for your hand, and wish for a better tomorrow.
But for all I know, our past is everything that I have of us and now, nothing else will follow

We've spent years together celebrating our birthdays and years have passed by since the last time we wished each other.
For all those years, that we spent apart, I hope your days were filled with laughter
But today,
I will light candles and blow a kiss to the sky, because I know you are there, I know you are….

Kavita Malviya

नारी - एक दिन की हकदार नहीं

तू फूल सी कोमल है,
तू पत्थर सी कठोर भी है।
तू परिवार के लिए झुकती है,
तू खुद के लिए झुकाती भी है।
तू शांत है, शीतल है,
और जरूरत पड़े तो आग भी है।
तू जड़ है किसी की,
तो दर्द की दवा भी है।
दूसरों के लिए जीए तो फ़र्ज़ है,
खुद के लिए जीए तो कर्ज है
तूने खुद को खो दिया है कहीं ,
तो तूने खुद के लिए जगह बनाई भी है।
तू किसी से ज्यादा नहीं,
तो तू किसी से कम भी नहीं है।
तू समानता की गुहार है,
लड़ना तो तुझे हर वक़्त ही है।

तू सिर्फ एक दिन की हकदार नहीं,
तू हर एक दिन की हकदार है।

I was struggling with my mind,
I was struggling for my inner peace.
I felt, I'm falling into a trap,
A trap of darkness,
Which I couldn't get out.
I felt, I'm drowning in a sea,
A sea of darkness,
Where I couldn't breath.
In the way, I was just struggling,
Struggling between
My soul and my body.
In the way , you came,
You came without hold my hand,
You got me out of that dark trap,
Saved me from that sea,
Showed me the beach,
Where i can breath freely.

But again, I started struggling,
Struggling between
My soul and my body.
This time I want,
I want, you hold my hand,
Across every struggle, with you.

First Love

I never know that one can fall in love easily but when I fall in love with that one person for the first time, I thought love is a miracle, love is something special and love is amazing. One day while I was going to temple, I saw him, that moment my heart skipped a beat I never know that feeling is love but I thought it's an attraction. Again, I saw him in a mall my heart skipped second time and the third time while I was spending me time in a coffee shop, he sat Infront of me and I am surprised at that time he asked can I talk with you and I said yes you can and he said I love you I was surprised and shocked and I said "yes" because every time I saw him I just fell in love with my own self and I think is love is all about loving yourself first. Whatever can happens in life but you never gonna miss your first love. First love teaches everyone a lesson no matter what it is. It's always precious.

Keerthana Suriya

Make Miracles Happen Through You

It's easy to dream about success
It's easy to give excuses and procrastinate
We are all good at it but
To become a successful person
We have to put efforts
We have to make moves,
We have to make changes
Step-by-Step in the right direction
Every ambitious person will have
a phase of fall
A phase of fall to strengthen the inner strength
Let go of the thoughts that make you weak
Don't give up
Overcome all the hurdles
A beautiful spring awaits at the end
Learn. Explore. Empower
Be Successful
MAKE MIRACLES HAPPEN THROUGH YOU

Another Bad Poem

I can never follow my dreams in my life
And I do not think that
I have knowledge and ability
Many people dislike or hate me
And I will never believe that
I will be helpful to anyone
I want to share with you that
In my future days
I will not be famous
I cannot even say that
My friends and family will help me
Am very confident that
Iam a fool
It's childish to assume that
I have goals in my life
My life is like a war
Without any dreams
Being successful is not my aim
Being happy is not in my destiny
I will never say that
I have a dream to follow in my life

(Now read from bottom to top)

Morph

Swollen eyes, pink red nose
Tears pattered on the floor;
Like a trampled rose.
She sat weeping in the corner, behind the door.

Between wrong and right, death and fear
His pillows soaked,
With tears of vengeance and abhor;
His feelings croaked.

Demise- their solution
For something so silly
Life is so not a fiction,
To end it so lowly.

Just open that door
To step out to the meadow,
Of happiness and warmth, love and care,
Your hiccups will then bow,
Miracles will thus show.

Monisha Ray

A Tiny Hope

Her eyes suddenly glowed up. The corner of her mouth drifted upwards, with dimples pressed under her cheekbone. Clapping and jumping a little, she ran towards the wooden door.

In every silence, in between each giggle, a distant rhythm could be heard with chasing wind.

It was the beginning of monsoon, and how eagerly the little girl was waiting for it as a fisherman waits with lure hanging from his fishing rod.

She could now sit for hours, watching the shiny drops shower over the petals of her favorite red hibiscus, planted just outside her tiny mud-house door.

She could mimic the jumping of frogs from grass to grass with their croaking sound.

She could see birds sheltering under dense branches fluffing up time to time.

She spread her fairly cold hand ahead, under the cloudy sky playfully to allow the raindrops to splatter on her bare palm.

"And there, she couldn't just stop smiling, after all the nature fulfilled a little heart's long longing hope."

Small Periods Of Rest

The time you acknowledge you have no one, not a single soul by your side, you just break down to the profundity, to the weakest point. You try to pick yourself up every damn time you fall, again and again. This won't stop until the day of your self-worth realization. You know you're capable of so many things that you can't even count. You are the brightest star of your own enchanted world. They say everyone has that one person in their life who's there, in the highs and the lows, through thick and thin and If you are blessed with someone like this you're lucky, but the truth is life is full of expectations and the worst-case scenario, when you are cursed with one. There come some days when you feel like laying in your bed all day long, doing nothing. No talking, no functioning, just a moment of introspection. This is when you discover that resting doesn't always slow you down, but the reverse. It makes you a better and stronger version of you. The 'you' that will be loved by you, respected by you, adored by you. So just sit down, relax and deal with your issues with small periods of rest. You will feel, then slowly, you will heal and the fire within you will now have more tendency to burn the negativities surrounding you.

Meenakshi Periyasamy

Secret Vice Of Love

My pity words kept bleeding
till unsettling dusk
met blinding dawn
In every vile drop
your miscreant name
found a way to be engraved
Unsaid goodbye meant
the beginning of painful era
Never defying his master,
this cruel enigma
became the crucifying saeculum
In the quest to imprison
thy fading footprints,
I found them fleeing
between my fingers
Amid this already lost
game of hearts
I lost the only path
left to collect
the remnants of me
Death laughed, as I have
become a living non-existent
Too numb that,
Love and pain made
heaven and hell indifferent

घर के लाल

यूँ तो सामाजिक तौर पर यह मान लिया गया है
कि स्त्री और पुरुष मे अब ख़ास अंतर नहीं
पर इस सामाजिक अवधारणा के पीछे छुपे झोल से हम सभी भली-भाँति परिचित हैं
रानी मुखर्जी जब एक साक्षात्कारी बातचीत मे कहती हैं,
"बराबरी तो दूर की बात है, हिस्सेदारी मिल जाए वही बहुत है"
यह सुन के अंतरमन मे चिंगारी सी उठ जाती है
ऐसा लगता है मानो किसी ने उन सारे पुरुष प्रधान लम्हों का, उन सारे पुरुष प्रधान वाक्यों का ,
तमाचा एक बार फ़िर जड़ दिया हो
एक बार फ़िर से पितृसत्ता माथे पर आ तांडव करने को तैयार है |
एक बार फ़िर औरत को multitasker
और पुरुष को घर के लाल जैसे शब्दों से नवाज़ा जाने वाला हो
घर के लाल,
जिनके आने पर समाज और घरों मे ढोल, नगाड़ों की गूंज उठने लगती है
जिनके आने पर छप्पन भोगों सा पकवान पूरे मोहल्ले को परोसा जाता है |
घर के लाल,
इनके दुनिया मे आते ही, इन्हें पितृसत्ता मे ढल जाना होता है |
ये बन जाते हैं माँ के लाड़ले और पिता का गुरूर,
बहन के मालिक और समाज के लिए एक आवश्यक ऊर्जा
जब ये शायद चलना भी नहीं सीख पाते, पूरा कुटुंब इनके पीछे चलना आरंभ कर चुका होता है
इनका घरेलू कामों से दूर-दूर तक कोई नाता नहीं होता
क्योंकि भैया! वो तो प्रकृति ने औरतों के लिए बनाये हैं न?

घर के, दुनिया के सारे ऐश-ओ-आराम सबसे प्रथम इन्हें ही नसीब होने चाहिए
घर की औरतों का खानपान इनके खानपान पर निर्धारित होता है
इन्हें घूमने की पूर्ण आज़ादी है पर इनके अनुसार औरतों के कदम घर के बाहर १०० शर्तों पर ही पड़ने चाहिए
फ़िर चाहे उन शर्तों पे ये लाल भले ही खरे ना उतरे क्योंकि, ये तो लाल है न, इन्हें गलती करने का हर अधिकार है
तभी इन्हें प्रेमिका चाहिए वेरोनिका जैसी और हमसफर मीरा जैसी
इन्हें प्रेम मे प्रेमिकाओं को ज़लील करने का भी अधिकार है
इनके विधुर होने पर, इन्हें तुरंत दूसरा ब्याह रचाने का भी अधिकार है
बलात्कार भी इन्हीं राड़ों के हाथों तो लिखा गया, रचा गया एक घिनौंना व्यवहार है
स्त्री पर ऊँची आवाज़ उठाना भी इनका एक बहुमुल्य अधिकार है
एक राह चलती स्त्री को असुविधा प्रदान करना,
उसके अंगों को छुना (उसकी इज़ाज़त के बिना) ही तो इनके अनुसार समाज मे क्रांति लाना है
इनके पास एक बहुमुल्य चीज़ होती है, अहंकार
अहंकार, जिससे हम सभी को भयभीत होना चाहिए
और हम होते भी हैं
तभी तो,
घर के और शायद समाज के इन लालों की बदौलत हमने समाज मे कई क्रांतियाँ देखी हैं
और आगे भी देखेंगे बेशक!

Fight for Cure

Cancer is only going to be a chapter in your life, not the whole story. Have you ever thought how would be the mind set of patients suffering from Cancer?
We all know about their physical sufferings but how would their mental health be?
Depression is the common psychiatric disorder in all cancer patients. The most essential medicine that must be given to them is 'Hope'. The journey they are on is purposeful and the struggles they undergo develop their strength.
"DIFFICULT ROAD OFTEN LEADS TO BEAUTIFUL DESTINATION"

Cancer is just a disease that comes like a passing cloud. It cannot cripple love. It cannot shatter hope. It cannot corrode faith. It cannot eat away peace. It cannot destroy confidence. It cannot reduce eternal life. It cannot quench the Spirit. .
They have only two options in life-1. Fight against Cancer. 2. Follow the first option

"This too shall pass"

Namisha Barik

"Her Life's Medicine - Love"

First this life of her was at death's door,
blind already and serene as demise,
snowflakes on her blossoms lying,
scarcely heaving with the puff .

Pure soul came by and having known her ,
in a dreamland of fables ,
gently ceased and laid upon her ,
mystiosalve of holy mits .

Intertwined fingers with folded eyelids ,
as the deep soft feel breathed ,
as smoothly as the heavenly deed ,
Through the epitome of his soul love .

So, when her life looked upward ,
being blissed and kindness from God ,
sight was with sweetness of his nectar ,
which was more than ever imagined .

Turning her life to be her choicest happiness ...But only love sight !

Neeraj kumar

1. My life is full of beautiful miracles
but it is the wish of God as he tackles
my work is just to take the life in every form whether you live in India or live in Rome

2. Till my fourteen I was unaware of poverty And there was a future without any surety
But I was heading towards an uncertain goal
In which I did not know even my role

3. Then I started my life with carrying weight on head
And in that phase every dream was totally dead
But along with this I was continue in my study
Only with poverty, pain but no friend or buddy

4. It was the bad phase of life as a labour Only sorrow, pain and compulsion were my neighbour
But at 16 I entered in the city college
That was the beautiful phase to increase my knowledge

5. Till here I had seen much more in my life
Sometimes it it was like a flower and sometime like a knife.
But now goddess Saraswati showed some pity.
And I made with my pains a beautiful treaty .

6. Now life was coming on track after facing many jackals .
And was showing again and again beautiful miracles.
Till now life has taken a meaning in deep .
And this journey called poverty to Principalship .

7. Now writing these words after becoming the principal
But miracles in life have become integral
Navneet Choudhury

"Let's Go !!!"

As drops combine, growing strength to strength,
Cutting through rocks, of every width and length,
Let's go to a place, to solace, as nature mourns,
Where nature nurtures and a river is born

As peaks touch into the never-ending sky
Infusing into each other, as they lie
Let's go to a place where heaven meets earth,
Where peace showers in solitude, in any company's dearth

As the sun fails to creep in, through its girth
But in its lap, half the world takes birth
Let's go to a place, where fauna meets flora,
Where the forest feeds us unlimited, us greedy remora.

As the water changes form, turning to ice,
When nature takes extreme form, yet a paradise,
Let's go to a place where snow covers all around,
Where the glaciers rest, with tranquillity abound,

As the water comes to kiss us on shore,
With the horizon leading onto heaven's door
Let's go to a place deep into the ocean,
Where peacefully we can enjoy the sun in motion

As wherever one can see, sand cover up the land,
With dunes in layer imitating the waves of sand,
Let's go to a place, far away in the depth of a desert,
Where every soul perishes, nature's own outskirt.

Let's go to a place to drench the soul in nature's lap
Where the soul reincarnates as a baby and enjoys the nap
Let's go to uncover the true inner self, from the façade
Where there's no end no beginning, no need for charade...

तुम नाराज हो जाती हो

तुम छोटी-छोटी बातों पर
नाराज हो जाती हो।
बस,बहाना चाहिए तुम्हें तो
रूठने के लिए,
कितनी प्यारी लगती हो,
जब तुम कहती हो कि 'मैं नाराज हूँ तुमसे"।
तुम गाल फुला लेती हो
और चेहरा अजीब-सा बनाती हो।
जब रूठता देखता हूँ,
छोटी-छोटी नन्ही-सी परियों को
तो तुम्हारी रूठने वाली बातें
मुझे याद आ जाती है।
मैं तुम्हें मनाता हूँ तो
तुम जल्दी ही मान भी जाती हो।
तुम छोटी-छोटी बातों पर
नाराज हो जाती हो।

'एक हक़ीक़त ज़िन्दगी की !'
कौन कहता है के मरने के बाद साथ कुछ नहीं जाता ;

Love Doesn't Stay

You used to call me "BAE"
You meant I'm most the important to you, Okay.
Later,
I got to know,
it was all just a Play.
I wasn't even a bit important to you,
but,
Even after all this,
in my heart,
my love for you still stayed,
But remember,
after a certain period of time,
Love doesn't stay,
it simply fades away.

बस चलते रहना है

मंज़िल तक पहोचने के रास्ते पर तुम्हें कई लोग मिलेंगे,

कुछ दोस्त के रूप में तो कुछ दोस्त का मुखौटा पहने हुए मिलेंगे,
कुछ मंज़िल तक पोहचाने में मदद करेंगे तो कुछ बस मदद करने का दिखावा करेंगे,
कुछ हमेशा साथ रहेंगे तो कुछ हमेशा साथ रहने के वादे करेंगे।

लोग चाहे जितने भी मिलें, जो भी मिलें, जहा तक साथ निभाएं, जहा पे छोड़ दें..
तुम्हे नहीं रुकना है, तुम्हे मुड़कर पीछे नहीं देखना है..
तुम्हे बस चलते रहना है, बस चलते ही रहना है।

कबतक?

तबतक जबतक मंज़िल पर पहोच नहीं जाते,
तबतक जबतक सब दुख भूल नहीं जाते,
तबतक जबतक मौत खुद तुम्हें आकर बुला नहीं लेती,
यानी तबतक जबतक है जान, तू मेरी बात मान,
कुछ नहीं करना है आए मुसाफिर,
बस चलते रहना है, जबतक है जान, जबतक है जान।

Do Miracles Exist??

I don't know if miracles exist
But I've seen the fallen to rise as if it was a bliss
If miracles are true tell them to bring back
Like the to lost comes back after a thousand impact

As if some miracle had helped them through the way
To regain the strength they needed for the day
For some, miracles cross the stone road
For some, they help themselves to overcome the load

To the miracle maker above the cloud
Listen to my prayers as I'm lost in the crowd
Miracles bring back the bed of the dead
Miracles have no explanation as they are not made

The homeless get shelter to give his tired body some rest
The hopeless get some reason to think that he is not any waste
Everybody wants something to happen which is best
And all I want is to get her back, it's just a request

She's gone, she left the world a few moments ago
Maybe she was needed up there, leaving me in the rough flow
I pray so a miracle may happen if I can also go
We were old, on our last day, and I don't want to grow old, no more

Wait, what happened suddenly, I see everything blur
Am I floating above? Am I going to her?
Yes, I see her shadow, waiting for me at heaven's door
I went to her, never felt so happy before
To meet my love in the afterlife, I really can't believe this
Yes, miracles do exists, as she welcomed me with a kiss

Payal Surani

Unconditional Love

"I am exhausted and you chose today to startle me. What was on your mind when you approved the plan of his?" She shouted in an arrogant tone.
"I am sorry, love. I was unaware of your condition. I wanted to surprise you with his plan. But you seem shocked actually." He let out trying to hide his smile.
"I totally comprehend what you are trying to hide." She narrowed her gaze towards him. He burst into laughter. Soon his laughter died down once he smelled her fury.
"I mean..." She didn't let him complete.
"Shut up. Help me in getting ready. We'll leave in an hour." She let out straight in a deciding tone.
Now it was his turn to get shocked. His mouth was wide open as she agreed to accompany him to his mate's place.
"You are a darling. I thought you would completely deny it." He said with a wide grin.
"How can anyone deny that puppy face?" She said playing with his cheeks.
"Let's make you prettier and leave." He said with a smile never leaving his face.

Pragathishri Sreedhar Shanthi

Childhood Memories

Generally, memory plays a important role in everyone's life. Memories are of different types

Good Memory
Bad Memory
Childhood Memory

Good memory gives a remarkable lesson for life. Bad memory gives a unforgettable lesson for life. But childhood memory gives a irreplacable lesson for life. In this story I am going to share some irreplaceable childhood memories.

In the year October 25, 1997. I was 3-year-old. October month was Diwali season. So my dad decided to celebrate Diwali with me. I too was so eager to celebrate Diwali. He gave me a cracker and he asked me to catch that cracker in my hand. Then he went to take candle and match box in room. I was standing with that cracker in my hand and thought that it was a lollipop given by dad and I swallowed that cracker. Then my dad immediately took me to the hospital and few doctors in the hospital saved me. But because of swallowing cracker my sweet voice changed.

when I was 5-year-old. I was playing with the sweet lemon seeds. Suddenly while playing I myself unknowingly inserted one seed in my nose . Then my mom tried so hardly to take that seed from my nose but she was unable to take that seed. Then immediately she took me to a ENT Specialist. Those doctors saved me.

Life is a Book where memory remains as a irreplaceable lesson.

If you remember the memorable irreplaceable experience that you get from your life then you will surely become a sportive person in future.

Riddhi Lodha

Today, we have a major part of the world's population facing the rage of depression,
Be the helping hand and caress them with protection.

SUICIDE PREVENTION MONTH. (September)

We have been taught "Slow and steady wins the race".
So let's strive together to erase the existence of this space.

Allow a person to feel all the emotions,
By keeping away your idea of "perfect life slogans".

If we shall practice being more empathic and less judgemental,
We will create a world full of potentials.

Attach these traits to your personality- kind and compassionate,
With which we shall be able to save our fellow passionates.

Ritika Sharma

The White Hue

In hues of shine,
In blues of divine,
Quenching for,
The taste of,
Never ending shrine...

Pondering over,
Curing the sick,
Fondling over,
Procuring the stitch...

Anticipating upon,
The dreams of her life,
In the fringe of pride,
residing in her mind...

Astonishingly,
A white coat ,
Now,
Hugs her all,
nursing the,
Baffled ones,
to an enlightened life.

What To Write

What to write when you don't feel like
When you lost your happy vibe
When you can't put your misery aside
When things don't seem right
When your own inner light is comparatively less bright
When your expectations and desire are not alike
When you can't find the words to define
The roaring thunder exist inside
It's possible when not giving up become your proudful choice
This way you can and always will win any battle of your life

Unbroken

Covered with dreary drapes, the veins in the body
Where the soul quivers to be unleashed
Held back with the black of the dead void
So much to say, so much to feel
Is available for the dreaded soul
What is to be done when the dreaded soul longs to be free

Free from the bondages, free from the shackles
The body keeps holding on
When will it let go?
When will the feels be not felt anymore?
The pain of life is not to be felt..
But now I'm beginning to relish it
Savour it and bring back my broken soul
To put up another fight
In the hope that it will come out
Unbroken, this time.

Rohit Lakhavatri

“Life is a one-man game; No one will accompany you. You born alone and you'll die alone only. In-between you strive hard to live your life at its best. And you cannot replace yourself; you have to play your own game. Others can just help you to make way for you while some will try to make you away from the game, Be aware of them!!”

“Being dark complexion isn't inferior. Instead take it positive as a blessing. Remember, The etymology of "Lord Krishna" which literally means Black, Dark and All Attractive with bliss. So being born as black is divine and you are fortunate of it!!”

“Fear is like your own shadow which appears huge to us than what actually it is; And it intensifies as you try to flee from it instead learn to fight against it so as to shine in dark or else it'll make you afraid of yourself.”

“Obama and Osama; The two most renowned names made by their own deeds. It's all up to you how you make your name by doing something virtuous or evil. The choice is yours!!”

“The STAR observed today was shone many years back; Keep your hardwork in persistent. It will outshine definitely not Today but Tomorrow.”

“Don't just beseech to god for elixir of your problems in your hard times. Also thank him for moments of happiness in your good times.”

“Until and Unless YOU yourself firmly stand on your own and move ahead. You will never find the way where you have to propel.”

Rohit Kumar

वीर जवान

अपने घर परिवार से दूर
सरहदों पर खड़े है बनके देश का नूर

बिना परवाह किए अपनी जान की
करते है रक्षा देश की शान से

सर्दी गर्मी चाहे हो बरसात
सरहद पर हमेशा रहते तैनात

पाक - चीन या नेपाल हमको आंख दिखाएंगे
हमारे वीर सिपाही उनकी आंख नोच लाएंगे

कारगिल के युद्ध में जवानों ने जान की बाज़ी लगाई थी
तब जाके पाकिस्तान को धूल चटाई थी

चाहे मिले, न मिले रोटी नून
फिर भी देश के लिए बहाते है अपना खून

देश का हर जवान अपना कर्तव्य निभाता है
तब जाके इस देश का व्यक्ति चैन की नींद सो पाता है।।

Roneeca Brajasundar Sahu

Quotes

1. Log sath nahi hue toh kya, unki yaad sath hoti hai.

2. Roshni toh har jagah hai, thodi si roshni zindagi mein bhi aa jaye.

3. Barish ki boonde kabhi kabhi gham bhula dete hai.

4. Kuch baatein kitabon mein hi kaid hoke reh jati hai.

5. Khudko aise chupaya ki tumhari khushi dekh sake.

Swati Pahad

मिलकर तुझे मैं तेरी लगी..

तु मुझको मिला ,कुछ ऐसे मिला
मिलकर मुझे तु मेरा लगा..
मैं तुझसे मिली ,कुछ ऐसे मिली
मिलकर तुझे मैं तेरी लगी..

तुने सबको चाहा ,मैंने तुझको चाहा
इस चाहत को मैंने दोस्ती कहा..
चाहत में तुने नाम किसी और का लिया
इस गम को मैंने पी भी लिया..

हर एक कदम पर संग तेरे चली
ऐसे ही अनजाने में तेरी हुई..
खुशी हुई ये रिश्ता बना
खुबसुरत अफ़साना बना..

मेरी शायरी के धागों में बांधे रखु
इस तरह से तुझे अपना कहु...
तुझसे मैं फिर मिल सकु ना सकु
मेरे दिल और दुआ में नाम तेरा लिखु...

तु मुझको मिला कुछ ऐसे मिला
मिलकर मुझे तु मेरा लगा..
मैं तुझसे मिली ,कुछ ऐसे मिली
मिलकर तुझे मैं तेरी लगी..

Samparnna Dalbehera

Last-Gasp To Back Alive: Miracles Happen

I was clued up of the happening of miracles. But didn't believed of its existence until that day when it happened to us. I didn't knew the power of miracles until that day when I was about to lose my father to acute hypertension rush and sugar drop. Once in a rainy morning, the person who used to get-up by 5:30 in the morning everyday without any fail , didn't wake up till 7. Me and my mother weren't surprised because he was unwell since few days. We thought that he must be sleeping due to ill- striken body. But no. He was frozen from tip to toe. The rate of heartbeats was lesser than normal seventy-two beats. We called up for few doctors but none came over due to heavy rain. Suddenly in a fraction of seconds his body was ice cold, completely collapsed. There was no more heartbeat, lungs about to collapse. At that point of time, we were confirmed that we lost him. But God had some different plans, he didn't let that happen. And to our surprise a doctor arrived with a pack of saline tube and a glass of sugar syrup. We were somehow hopeless. But hopes never goes to vain. With the moment of few minutes he responded to stimulus. He woke up from his death bed and said "Why are you all crying, I am not dead yet, I am born to lead a longer life, longer than before". We were awestruck gazing at him. That was no less than a miracle, right? That's how from that day, I believed in the power of Almighty and power of miracles. Miracles does happen not just ones but many a times. Sometimes we are aware and sometimes not.

Shijin Ravi C

My Last Wish

It rained and rained.
Without an endless clue.
No thunder but lighting.
Everything was then dusty.
No trees no houses nor any sole.
All vanished in thin air.
With piece mind and a cup tea.
Sucked the sip loved the drops.
Nowhere was nature so beautiful.
Like a diamond bloom.
With sun with par light.
I wondered in all alone.
What a day and what a moment.
Many questions to unsolved .
Yet a thousand piled up aside.
Next moment a breeze woke me up.
It was my mind working .
And all near it was a cute miracle.

Subhransu Padhy

।। सूर्योदय ।।

मेरे लिए तो सूर्योदय
उम्मीदों से भरा भंडार है,
उसके किरणें मेरे लिए ऐसा है
मानो मेरी प्रेरणा का संसार है।

जब खुद को अकेला या टूटता हुआ
महसूस करू खिड़की के पास जाकर बैठता हूँ,
उगता हुआ सूरज रोज़ सीख दे जाता है मुझे संघर्ष की...
तब मैं फिर खुद को संभालता हुआ लौटता हूँ।

हो सकता है यह सूर्योदय और सुबह की
किरणें दूसरों के लिए सामान्य हो,
पर मुझे सदा ये खिड़की का
प्रतिबिंब से चैन पहुंचाते हैं,
जब भी याद करता हूँ अपनी प्रियतमा को..
भाँति भाँति यह प्रतीक बनने लगते हैं।

सुबह की रोशनी इन खिड़कियों से प्रेरणा लेती है,
आने वाले कल को एक नई ऊर्जा दे जाती है,
विश्व में इतने अंधकार के बावज़ूद
भी चमकना है हमें कैसे सितारों की तरह...
हर एक किरणें वह पत्ते पर
मुझसे यह बात याद दिला जाती है।

Miracles

I believe in miracles,
Because it gives me hope.
No matter how strong are rivals,
It makes your winning scope.

It is said by somebody,
When you are at the end of rope.
Tie a knot,
But don't lose your hope.
But yeah, Miracles don't exist,
For them who are lazy.
Miracles work for them,
Who works for it like crazy.

Saptak Baral

Walk with me
Holding my hand
Along the wet sand
Beside the sea.
Feeling my soul
In every breathe.
Let me dive into you
Until dawn kisses
The earths feet.

Alone

Nobody helps,
When you have no power.
But
One thing which helps u,
your determination to face it alone.

Sybil Samuel

Image

She was speechlessly staring herself
In the mirror. . .
Pale, lifeless, her eyes lacking luster
She was once known "miss beautiful hair"
Her eyes were wet as she stares the girl in the mirror ..
She lost her lovely, silky black tresses ...
There was a girl standing ... Bald, frail, her skin appearing dull,
Eyes saggy due to lack of sleep
She looked at her image and cried
And cursed herself... Her fate ...
Chemotherapy turned her into a vulnerable, weak and ugly figure
She questioned her mom,
"do you think i'm pretty?"

Her mother without a thought to pause
Smiled at her and said "you are my princess "
"nothing can ever change who you are"
Her heart melted and so did all her insecurities

Sukrurtha B

You mean a lot more to me.
I believed in miracles because of you;
You are the miracle;
You are the magic;
You are all the marvel in my life.
I love you more and I will always want to be a part of your magic.

अर्णव - 'एक लक्ष्य'

अपनी सोच को एक दिशा देने में कार्यरत हूं
रास्तों पर नजाने कई अंगारे हैं परिचित हूं
लक्ष्य निर्धारित है सकारात्मक सोच रखता हूं
आत्मविश्वास दृढ़ सामर्थ्य में अपने केंद्रित हूं।

अपनी योग्यता का बखान नहीं करना चाहता
एक ख़ुशबू लेकर चारों और संक्रमित हूं
जीवन रूपी सागर में तैरना सीख रहा हूं
थोड़ा कठिन मगर विचारों पर सटीक हूं।

चैतन्य को मैंने आंतरिक रूप से धारण किया है
क्षमता को एक पायदान देकर चल रहा हूं
मंजिल कितनी दूर है मापना जायज़ नहीं समझा मैंने
सपनों को वास्तविकता देने के लिए मचल रहा हूं।

Shobika Balaraman

Why I breathe?

The torment of my art
Wane in thine grin,
The wail of my soul
Calm in thy warmth,
The dense of my notion
Vanish in thine sight,
The mass of my dolour
Split asunder by thy leela,
And coz of thine heed
In the murk of my voice,
I breathe, thou divine.

Sandhya A. S.

I Accept Your Offer...

I accept your offer...
Not because you started hating me
But because I started loving you more
Even if accepting it will lead to my destruction.
One last time!
And you will say adieu to your lost love
And I will water it once again
In hope of redeeming it to life.
But in vain, but to avail no fruition.

Feckless thoughts, incarcerated dreams and
Vanishing hopes of tomorrows.
Past was it.
Why didn't it witness our present?
Only I was there, in search of you
Amidst drops of crimson anguish
Falling on the sand castle of ours.

I accepted your offer once.
And dedicated my life for it.
I don't know when the red rose
Gave way to sweet briar
And to bitter one.
Curly hair aroused your amusement no more.
Caressing touch of mine was turned down to rest.
Discussions tasted demise.
Only shouting prevailed.

Yet, why my tears reflect the sweet old him still?
Why I yearn for his presence to continue for ever?

Why I struggle to regain my consciousness only to see him?
Why I want a rebirth from the sustained death only to love him?
Alas! My soul lurks in the darkness of valley of my dreams.
Yes, I accept your offer...

Express

Express!!!
Express it all.
Express your
feelings of emotions,
anger and love,
or whatever remains
in your heart.
Don't wait for a miracle
to happen but remember
efforts is all that matters.
Express it with the person
who is with you.
Else you will only be
left with "guilt"
when that person will
no more be with you or
may not survive anymore.
So it's up to yourself
whether you choose
to express or guilt.

Life Is Beautiful

Life is beautiful when you are with me
Life is beautiful when you smile
My heart is beautiful when you stay in it
I can't imagine my life without you
You make my life beautiful
Life is meaningful when you laugh
Life is wonderful with you my love
You are the treasure of my life
My love you are the reason for my life
Life is beautiful when you are around me
Life is beautiful with you one day
Life is beautiful when you love
I love this beautiful world when you beside me
Life is beautiful when dream come true
Life is beautiful with you my love
I can't imagine my life without you ...

I Want Your Love....

I want only your love
I want late night talks
I want late night walks
I want only your smile
I want your trust
I want to be always by your side
I want to be the one who's always there to hold you in the dark
I want with you endless talks
At the end I only want you
The one who loved you from the very start..

चाहता है

कुछ ख़ास कर जाने का जज़्बा सा है
पर उसे देखे बिना
अब कुछ रास कहां आता है

कुछ बातें मन में बसी है
उससे कहने को भी दिल घबराता है
कैसे कहूं उसे

उसकी आंखों में डूब जाने को दिल चाहता है,
उसकी बातों मैं खो जाने को
दिल चाहता है,
दिल चाहता है जी लू इश्क़ में उसके
चाहता है, चाहता है, चाहता है, ये
दिल सिर्फ उसको ही चाहता है।

Shreyas Sahay

A Girl I Met in High School

A girl I met in high School,
Pure innocent but not fool,
Obscure of the path to choose,
Oblivious to talks that are loose,
Resilient to all falls and crooks,
Voluptuous is the word for her looks.
Abiding love for her family,
Known best for treating people kindly.
Affable approachable and addictive,
Shyness is essence of her being seductive.
Happiness is all she distributes,
Yappy she, likes him to be mute.
All about this girl in high school,
Pure innocent but not fool.

Miracle

Happens suddenly,
Happens unexpectedly,
Either good or bad,
Good Brings delight;
It clears the clusters,
Bad vanish the faith;
Further, gives tears
Never depend on miracle,
Build yourself up,
You are your Own Savior,
Fight yourself in your battle,
Your miracle is Your Success,
Your field is your Race,
Your faith is your boost,
Your goal is your victory

Shubham

Affection Everlastingly

I 'm limited everlastingly by your affection;
My heart can hear everything your eyes says;
Your appeal is what I'm pulled in to,
I'm happy we are at long last together my adoration;
Your adoration to me is the most valuable blessing;
Without you I would never have found this second;
I love you my dear and I will consistently,
Remain next to you and never at any point leave you;
Your unadulterated heart transmits hopeful vibes;
It generally lights up my spirit and my faculties;
I guarantee I'll never make you extremely upset,
Also, I can't actually envision myself without you ;
I feel I'm the most fortunate individual ever ;
To encounter the magnificence of genuine romance and sentiment ;
Our excursion together has quite recently started ;
The best beginning to an affection life one can actually envision ;
I express gratitude toward God for the most lovely creation on this world ;
I'm ever going to observer for an amazing duration ;
My lone desire is to remain with you perpetually ,
What's more, consume my time on earth with you together till the end ;
Since I love you everlastingly ......

Shivansh Mishra

Your Words

Violets are red Scarlets are blue
Meet my mornings , I swear it's true
I live in meadows but the sky is often dark
I don't live in a treehouse but my walls look like bark

I keep resting my head on it , gives me some sort of comfort
Must be the roughness , don't you know , it's like some sort of dirt
The dirt you rub on your wounds and call yourself a man
It burns through your veins but revives your spirits, yes you can

I rest my head , to my conscious self i see
Lying there , agitated ,right in front of me
I am me , but I can see me , I know it's insane
It's cruel , it feels so , to watch myself in pain
And right at the moment I feel like i will burst
I scream in laughter and suddenly it would rain

The rains bring more laughter , does wash away the dirt.
But if one drop brings relief the other one would still hurt.
When the clouds as dark as my anxiety would leave the open ground

Yes you you heard correctly, not sky, that's how shadows hover around
When the clouds as dark as my anxiety would leave the open ground
They would bring the brightest sun all thirsty and round
This sun as it sounds is not a hint of hopes

It would burn on my wounds like the friction of a thousand ropes
And after it has burnt all the venom ,that creeps to my bone I still feel more hurt than my dear one , you will feel on my tombstone.
The dirt is my ego, the laughter is my limit
The rain are my tears, watching one my spirit
The sun is you forgetfulness, venom were my efforts
But what took me to my grave weren't my deeds but your words.

Swapnali Jagtap

आसान नही है जिना फिरभी जिने लगी थी ...
अपनोंका साथ हैं ये पाकर मै उभरी हुई थी ....
क्या कहु मै किसिसे ,
कोन जान पाया मुझे...
बस अब खतम हूआ है सिलसिला
ना अब कोई चाहत है..
ना ही आसुओं का झिलमिलाना

S. K. Vishnu Prasath

The Will

A gusty warrior moving ahead in this cruel world,
With the hope for the glorious light,
Yet he stood in the fight,
He trembled through the sorrows and regrets,
Carrying his people in his heart,
The vilant gave up all he brought,
Wearing courage and nothing,
The vision he had made him firm,
And the love he had filled his heart till brim,
Struggling with the way that made him to bleed,
He clenched his fist against everyone's greed,
The ray of hope never let him down,
And the ever-ending courage gave him the crown.

THE TIME

Time changed everything,
Bodies grew old,
Whereas the heart stayed gold,
The feeling we inhumed got provoked,
To find the right one to express.

Miracles

A miracle is often defined as being a supernatural act or an act of God. Sometimes it is more specifically and negatively defined as a violation of a natural law. In philosophy class we discussed different philosophers' views on miracles. David Hume's critique of miracles included the criterion that for something to be deemed a miracle, there must be substantial group of credible witness to attest to its occurrence.

Hume believes miracles do not exist. If something of the supernatural does happen it is not really supernatural it is part of nature, we just don not experience it often so we consider it to be supernatural or a miracle. Kant believes miracles have no role to play except in the rise and spread of a religion. Kant says miracles have no role to play in validating a religion since the truth of religion can be supplied by reason alone.

The difference between Kant and Hume is that Kant resists the idea that of some invisible agent.'In my opinion I believe that a miracle is an event that cannot be explained for by scientific reasoning, and so we do not understand why and how it has happened.

This could be due to the fact that we do not have the scientific knowledge and understanding to fully be able to explain it as even today we are learning knew things about the world around us.

People interpret miracles differently; some may believe that they have been performed by some higher power, such as Jesus, Allah and other religious Gods. Others just simply believe that miracles are not miraculous at all and are just showing that we do not fully understand everything about the world around us.

A Scenarios that happened in my Life i,e is The Miracle in my life There where clear blue skies and the sun had just stopped shining brightly as it prepared to go down as the evening grew

closer. I had been skiing and was enjoying myself. As I had found out later though, I had received much more then I had bargained for. At the time I was just relaxing and having a ordinary time. I was skiing by myself when it started to get dark out and that's when it all happened. I was skiing a routine run and minding my own business when a out of control snowboarder came crashing into me. I had lost both my skis and was tumbling down the mountain and I couldn't stop. Then finally I had stopped rolling down the mountain, but to my surprise I had learnt that the only reason I had stopped was because my ski boot was stuck in a pipe. during the summer when the snow had melted it had turned into a water park) I couldn't free my trapped leg of the pipe. I grew weary, as nightfall was almost here my instincts told me to head for shelter and spend the night on the mountain. Then I had realized that my leg was still caught in that pipe! Nightfall came shortly after. I thought to myself what if I wasn't found? what will I do? I was thinking a million thoughts per second, what if, how bout , but why... and that's when it hit me. I had encountered a near death experience and if on that day I hadn't made it out of there alive who would of even cared? I had then realized on that day who and what actually mattered to me. Anyway back to the story. Well...

I believe there are miracles in everyday living. For example take the miracle of life. Life is precious in every way possible. God putting us on this planet in his image is another miracle. We shouldn't take the precious gift of life that he gave us for granted. Another miracle is the miracle of conception. Children are what I believe we are to God and in return I believe that God wanted us to have our own children so that we could know what it feels like to have something so precious and so inoccent. We can hold a precious little miracle as dear to us as we are to God himself. There are many miracles around us; one just has to look closely. Another miracle would be the miracle of love. From personal experience I know love does exist. Love is a very powerful force. Love is a miracle that surprises everyone everyday. Life and love are two very powerful miracles in everyday life that we don't really see as miracles.We take so much for granted. Miracles are

Gods' way of saying I am here, you're not alone, and I am protecting you always. Miracles are everywhere at every second of the day. I believe Jesus did walk on water and he did turn water into wine, and they were big miracles in history, but the everyday miracles are what make the heart believe. The little miracles like hugs, kisses, and a voice saying "I love you." Those are miracles. Friends are a true miracle. They are there for you when you're having a horrible day. Friends will never leave your side when you're hurting. There is also the miracle of hugs, when you' re down. When you get hugged, it's a powerful force. When you recieve a hug, you suddenly get overwhelmed in an ocean of emotions. You feel safe, loved, wanted, and you get the feeling that you are important. Also a kiss is one special little miracle. A kiss in its own way can make you feel as if you're floating in air. A kiss from that special someone can make your mind wander away from all the stress in the world. A kiss can make you fly any where you want to go. But, words, "I love you" are the best miracle of all. When that special someone says, "I love you" you get butterflys in your stomach.

When they say "I love you," you get the urge of wanting to be with that person all the time. Love is a powerful magic, force, and miracle. I believe that God put love on this earth for a purpose, and this purpose is for us to know what he feels when he looks down on us from above.

The way we look at our children might be the way he looks upon us – with love. Little miracles are everywhere. One just has to look for them. I believe in the miracle of love.

A GREATFUL HEART IS A MAGNET FOR MIRACLES

Hatred

Thousands of reasons to love,
Yet a single piece of hatred diminished souls who tried best:)
Not necessarily meant to shower and glow?
But writings hidden alive in form of attachments are healing her to grow best,
And maybe on worst,
Sucks to express and feel love again!
Dilemmas sucks so hard, even waves of love can't comfort and console her mind to be once again loved and carry the immense purity within her heart.
As of now, living is just a part of her life! But struggles ahead will make her survive no matter, and with joy and enthusiasm.

Love Falls Apart

This short story is based upon the social conflict between the families of two lovers living in the small town of Kashmir. Somehow it is filled with autobiographical elements too. It was a young beautiful lady living in the small town of Kashmir along with her royal family. Which is surrounded with hills and dense forest. The family consists of Ammi, Abu, brother and three sister's. Among them fatima is the eldest one. Fatima is so beautiful with charming face and golden hairs. She was doing B. S. C from govt women's college .she has many admirers since form her school days among them one was her own cousin Junaid. But Fatima falls for the one who was beneath her class.Ali a middle class young man who was doing the job of teacher in local private public school. The love story between the two reaches at the climax. Fatima after completing her B. S. C takes admission in sate university (Kashmir university) where from she competed Her masters degree in literature. In university Fatima makes her relationship with Adnan. Though it was not for a long time. Ali reveals the truth after 6months.this was the beginning cause for the separation of two lovers. Fatima after completing her master's degree arrived home where she convinced again Ali .at the Same time Fatima's parents becomes aware about the relationship between the two. They warns Fatima to make distance from Ali as there was a social gap between them. Also, the dispute occurs between the two families regarding the same matter. Fatima takes the decision of going outside state for her 3-year research program. It was difficult for her to move on. Although there was no contact between them. But, she was still waiting for Ali.in between three years Fatima's family shifts permanently themselves towards new model

town. When Fatima arrives home after 2years.she reavels That Ali is now engaged with someone else. It was an unbearable pain for Fatima. Still Fatima was waiting for Ali. after six months Ali gets married with her friend Zeenat. Fatima now takes the decision of getting married with her own cousin Junaid who was once her admirer also. The love story of Fatima and Ali gets end after getting married. Now, both the lovers are permanently separated from each other.

My Pen and Her Beauty

Finally, I saw her pretty beautiful face,
Seems like she is ace of spades,
So perfect is the beauty of her face,
I thank god for such a peculiar face.

After seeing her pretty beautiful face,
Seeing her in each posture everywhere,
Not noticing her is rarest of rare,
If she is ready to talks and share,
Blessed to have her light and beauty which is so fair.

She is like a lovely charming moon,
Earlier I thought moon only shone in June,
Now I watch the sky every day,
And wait for the passing of moon.

Actually, she is beyond beautiful and cute face,
Let me say " fire",
But she is beyond everyone's reach,
So not everyone can " desire" for her.

Flairs and Glairs, a platform by a student for the students. We are esteemed youth struggling to carve out our path for our future and we follow a basic mindset Since everyone is not born with all-round skills. Joining hands with people who are born to execute it with perfection is the best way to evolve. Self-Evolution is the need of the hour but, evolving as a community is what we strive for. The initiative as kickstarted by, Founder- Mr. Shubham Shah with the motive to utilize the skillset and talent of writing has now a team of 10+ people who are actively participating into newer forms of learning and discovering talents among youngsters. We Provide platform and services like Publishing opportunities, Open mics, Workshops, Hands-on training. Operating with Brand Name of Flairs and Glairs (Publication House), we offer the chance of elevating a passionate writer to an esteemed author With Brand name Teekhe Zasbaaat. We bring to you an opportunity to get accustomed with the Public Speaking and Presenting of Thoughts along with regular challenges to brush up your inking spirit. The newest initiative to extend our services we introduced in a new writing Platform- The Glittering Fables and Ink Over Tears.

We Choose to Fly Like A Falcon than to be a Leg Pulling Crab.

To Know More: Infoline – 7781900870
Mail Us At-
flairsandglairs@gmail.com / info@flairsandglairs.in
Or Visit is at
www.flairsandglairs.com / www.flairsandglairs.in
Social Handles- @flairsandglairs @teekhezasbaaat

www.ingramcontent.com/pod-product-compliance
Ingram Content Group UK Ltd.
Pitfield, Milton Keynes, MK11 3LW, UK
UKHW022003190726
13853UKWH00004B/1714

9 789390 416004